A REVELATION OF OUR SAVIOR

A Revelation of Our Savior

WITH TRANSLATION AND COMMENTARY BY DR. MICHEL S. CURLLEN

H. Dean Fisher

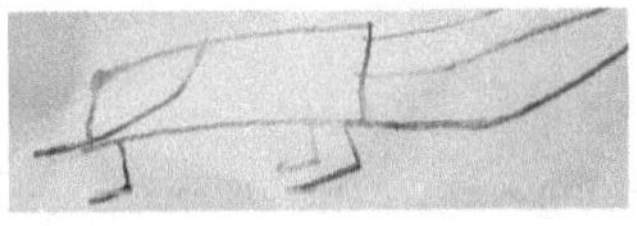

Seventh Battle Publishing

Cover illustration by Lily Guziewicz - lilyguziewicz.com
Author photo by John Kilker – JohnJKilker.com

Visit the website and sign up for the email newsletter:
HDeanFisher.com

Follow H. Dean Fisher on social media:
Facebook: www.facebook.com/SeventhBattlePublishing
Twitter: @HDeanFisher1
Instagram: HDeanFisher

Printed in the United States of America

First Mass Market Paperback Printing: February 2022
First Hardcover Printing: January 2021
Seventh Battle Publishing
Nicholson, PA, United States

Mass Market Paperback ISBN-978-1-952811-10-4
Ebook ISBN-978-1-952811-04-3

Contents

Author's Notes   ix

Dedication   x

1

The Find   1

    1   A Personal Note from H. Dean Fisher   2

    2   9

    3   16

    4   24

    5   31

    6   37

    7   43

    8   48

    9   52

2

The Revelation of Simon, Son of Cuphythis 57

10	The Revelation of Simon Chapter 1	58
11	The Revelation of Simon Chapter 2	61
12	The Revelation of Simon Chapter 3	66
13	The Revelation of Simon Chapter 4	71
14	The Revelation of Simon Chapter 5	76
15	The Revelation of Simon Chapter 6	82
16	The Revelation of Simon Chapter 7	89
17	The Revelation of Simon Chapter 8	92
18	The Revelation of Simon Chapter 9	99
19	The Revelation of Simon Chapter 10	103
20	The Revelation of Simon Chapter 11	108
21	The Revelation of Simon Chapter 12	113
22	The Revelation of Simon Chapter 13	116

3

Commentary & Analysis   **121**

---

23   Commentary & Analysis Prologue   122

24   Commentary & Analysis Chapter 1   127

25   Commentary & Analysis Chapter 2   136

26   Commentary & Analysis Chapter 3   149

27   Commentary & Analysis Chapter 4   157

28   Commentary & Analysis Chapter 5   164

29   Commentary & Analysis Chapter 6   175

30   Commentary & Analysis Chapter 7   184

31   Commentary & Analysis Chapter 8   189

32   Commentary & Analysis Chapter 9   195

33   Commentary & Analysis Chapter 10   203

34   Commentary & Analysis Chapter 11   207

35   Commentary & Analysis Chapter 12   212

36   Commentary & Analysis Chapter 13   215

37   Commentary & Analysis Epilogue   219

About The Author   222

Author's Notes

This book is divided into three sections: Dr. Curllen's discovery of this Revelation and the other ancient documents; Dr. Curllen's translation of the Revelation; and Dr. Curllen's commentary on the Revelation. Enjoy the end of the world as we know it.

Special thanks to my trauma advisor, Dr. Mark Hall; my publishing advisor, Ann Lavendar, www.AnnLavendar.com; and every end-times preacher who ever left me terrified at the conclusion of his sermon because the world was going to blow up tomorrow.

For those so inclined, the soundtrack to A Revelation of Our Savior is:

Jimmy Buffett, "A White Sport Coat and a Pink Crustacean"

Steve Taylor, "Meltdown (at Madame Tussauds)"

Shelley Segal, "Strange Feeling"

Beth Hart & Joe Bonamassa, "Seesaw"

This book is dedicated to all those seeking the truth. May its double-edged sword set you free.

1

The Find

1

A Personal Note from H. Dean Fisher

Dr. Michel S. Curllen doesn't exist. I made up the name. In fact, anyone who knows me well enough should be able to tell immediately that the name is fake. I did that to protect the identity of my childhood friend – the person who first brought this story to me. I also won't reveal my friend's gender. I'll call him a man for simplicity's sake, and I will leave the "Dr." in front of his name to accurately denote the Ph.D. he worked so hard to achieve. I don't want to make it too easy, though, for the people trying to hurt "him" to figure out who he is or where he is just because he knows me, so please understand that some of my information about him is meant to obscure his identity.

And yes, I truly believe there are evil forces in the world trying to hurt my friend. He came to me more than a year ago and asked for my help. I didn't believe him at first, but it didn't take me long to realize he was telling the truth. He had found something awesome in the wilderness of Romania.

Now, you might be the type of person to doubt me – you might be a "Doubting Thomas," as it were, the person who insists you won't believe unless you can see it for yourself. Touch it for yourself. Read it for yourself. That's good. That was me too. When Michel first texted me, I didn't believe it was really him, and I ignored him. Nearly blocked his number, but I didn't. I'm glad I didn't because she has something extraordinary to show the world – I know because he showed me.

After that first text, he sent me one more that contained a moment from our childhood, something we had done together when we were young and foolish. A memory that only he and I would know because no one else was there when we engaged in that activity, and so I could believe it was really him. That's when he had my attention, and that's when he told me his story.

We'd lost touch with each other decades ago when we each moved – me just around the bend, but Michel all the way across the country. (It was pre-internet, in case anyone is confused about how we lost touch with each other so easily.) He got serious about his schooling, got a great degree from a fantastic university, and – by all measures – had a great career as a teacher and researcher. Sadly, he lost it all – just because of this one particular discovery.

This is the thing: Dr. Michel S. Curllen found something that was never meant to be found. He found a treasure trove of scrolls and documents from thousands of years ago, and those documents have the potential to shake up religion. To shake up Christianity, and probably Islam and Judaism as well. Probably to shake up the entire world if he can ever get them all out there. He sent me the pictures, and even though I don't have a degree in archaeology or anthropology or whatever, I could tell that these things were ancient and important.

After those first few pictures he sent me some of the translations, and that's when I really realized how valuable this information could be and how important it was for the world to know. This first scroll contained some wild, new information about the mindset of 1st-century Christians. If you thought John's Revelation from the New Testament was mind-blowing, you'll be astounded by this "Revelation of Simon" – whoever he was. To see what I mean, here's a small section from the first chapter:

5. I, Simon, your brother and fellow traveler in the Way, was lost with a downcast heart at the Desolation we witnessed on Mt. Sinai.

6. The Lord let loose His wrath at the stubborn and wicked generation, striking down the ones who committed adultery with the Golden Calf.

7. They were blinded and could not seek out the serpent to cleanse them from their wickedness and unrighteousness.

8. They were swallowed whole by the Earth, never again to find solace at the feet of the Lord our God.

9. It was with crushing vindication that the Lord wiped away the memories of their hard hearts, of the disloyalty they showed to Him all the short days of His time with us.

Or this from chapter 2:

14. The desert fell away at my feet, and I was left walking through what had once been the Jordan River.

15. It was now a dry bed, parched and cracking in the heat of the noonday sun.

16. Bones were scattered all around, the bones of the witnesses and the shards of the twelve lampstands.

17. The earth shook as a mighty wind pounded the bones and the shards with the force of a thousand storms, lightning leaping into the sky, and the heavens clapping with the joy of righteousness.

18. The One who walked before me continued on as a second wind pounded the earth, the bones and the shards jumping into the air and falling back again.

19. At the third strike of the wind, the air grew still, and the bones floated as dust to the ground.

20. The shards of the twelve lampstands had become as a million tongues of flame scattered throughout the river bed.

Heady stuff, I know. Important to us all.

I should also mention that Dr. Curllen almost backed out of this publishing deal at the very last minute. He approached me with these pictures and his translations last year, and he asked me to help him bring it all to light. We texted for several weeks. Everything was on track, but then he had a run-in with some members of the organization that's trying to suppress this publication – the "Gnostic Brocade," as he calls them. They hid these documents centuries ago – blanketed them beneath the earth, you could say – and they did not want any of these documents coming to light now. They're the people who have been trying to stop Dr. Curllen – trying to hurt him or even kill him to keep these documents from being published. His close call with them in North Dakota really shook him, made him doubt his resolve to get these documents published.

I assured him, however, that it would all be worth it in the end. That he would be safer for these documents becoming public, and that nothing would happen to me as happened to so many of Dr. Curllen's family, friends, and colleagues. It would be difficult for me to simply "disappear," and so we must ensure his documents – the Dornisoara Scrolls as he calls them – get published.

He and I have established several secret ways of communicating, a few digital and physical dropboxes set up on the internet and around the country. This is only the first of many documents Dr. Curllen plans to translate, and he intends to produce a commentary on each one, just as he's done with this first Revelation – assuming he remains safe. I pray every day that he remains safe.

So please, read and enjoy Dr. Michel S. Curllen's exploits in his own words. After that, you'll be amazed at the text of this "Revelation of our Savior," and even more amazed at Dr. Curllen's commentary on his own translation. I think you'll agree that this is something truly remarkable, and the world must be informed.

2

My name has been assigned Dr. Michel S. Curllen. You should know from the start, however, that that is not my real name but a pseudonym provided by my friend and colleague, the person who meant so much to me in my younger days. I am writing this document and making sure that it gets published because I believe the world must know what I know no matter who wants me dead for knowing it and spreading it to the world. What you will read in this text is unbelievable. What I have to tell you, however, you must believe because it is so important to the foundation upon which all Christianity has been built.

I found something. Those three words, however, so completely fail to convey the absolute magnitude of what has been found as to make all the words in the English language inadequate. I find myself now in possession of a cache of secret documents that were hidden away by members of a religious sect more than 1,900 years ago. I have painstakingly spent the past several months translating only one of these documents, and I can assure you that this find is one of the biggest that we have ever had. This find makes the Nag Hammadi texts, the Dead Sea Scrolls, a mere pittance upon academic work. This find has the potential to completely rewrite our understanding of first century Christians, Jews, and all of life within the Middle Eastern portion of the Roman Empire. And I can say this all after translating only one of the texts. That is how important this find is to the entire world.

However, there are dangerous forces working against me to keep this information from being disseminated. In the past couple years of escaping with these documents I have come under extreme personal torture. My colleagues have abandoned me. My family has been taken from me. I find myself alone in the world in the icy cold and dark with the deaths and blood-soaked Earth. To say that I have dealt with despair throughout this time is an understatement. It is only the work of this translation and my renewed faith in God that has kept me going to this point. I find myself now with renewed purpose, and I don't believe I can be overstating the case when I say that I feel like one of the prophets of old. I am no longer myself.

There are so many people who have helped me in one way or another over the past couple years that to list them all would take the entirety of this text. Allow me at this point to simply thank those whom I can thank from my immediate vicinity. You will understand when I say that I am reluctant to thank these people by name for fear that they will come to some of the same horrifying episodes that have plagued me for the past few years. I would not wish my own personal hell upon any of these wonderful souls. I would not wish it even upon my worst enemy. Having said that, I want to thank my wonderful new colleague in Florida. At great risk to herself she was able to confirm through carbon-14 testing for me the dates of these documents. Maybe one day we can share the actual report that she created from her computer systems, the reports that so beautifully detail the date of this document, but to do so now would only put both of our lives in jeopardy. Please know that when I say these texts that I have found date back to the latter half of the first-century, please know that I say that with all scientific certainty based upon the work my colleague did on my behalf at great personal risk to herself. Again, I thank you.

I owe so much thanks to my friend who smuggled me out of Romania. That tale alone was harrowing, and I had every conviction I would not live to see the next day, but at great personal risk to himself and to his family, he saw me safely across the border and on to my next destination. At one point in that long journey, we nearly lost this entire treasury of documents, but he saw us through.

Thank you also to my priest friend, the man who personally led me from the forest in which I despaired and brought me out to the other side to find shelter and a family willing to take me in. That one family led me to so many more families who all saw the value of these documents and recognized the necessity of making them public, and they helped me move forward, onward to the next safe home, and the next, and the next, until finally I even found myself in the welcoming home of an atheist family that also saw the necessity of the translation and publication of these documents.

I must also give a sincere and heartfelt thank-you to my most personal friend, H. Dean Fisher. I worry about him, just as worry for you, dear reader, and just as I now worry for my colleague in Florida and my friends throughout Western and Eastern Europe, but he has assured me he is willing to take the risk, that the world must know of this important find, and he is willing to take the risk for my sake. For humanity's sake.

To best understand this important find, you must also understand me and who I am and how I got to be where I am, which, unfortunately, I cannot reveal for fear for my own safety. Though I was born in the United States, my parents were not, and that disconnect has remained a part of who I am to this day. I was always a part of the people around me, but I was also always separate from them, apart from them. There was a distance between me and them. It was the little things that added up to that big distance. The people who had trouble pronouncing my name. The way my skin color was not like the skin color of those around me. The jokes that the people around me would tell, that everyone else would laugh at, but I would not laugh at those jokes because I did not understand what made them funny. I did not understand the culture behind them. I know that now, though I was confused and resentful and a little hurt back then.

It seems only appropriate and somehow ironic that my life at the moment should so mirror my life from back then. I am once again the stranger in my own homeland, the outcast, the one who does not belong, but it is not the color of my skin or the accent when I speak or the way I do not understand people's jokes. No, I have now been forced to become the outcast. My family has been taken from me, my friends have been ostracized from me, and my colleagues have been threatened harm, either harm to their careers or to themselves or even to their families. I am at once a stranger in my own land and a fugitive from those who might best be able to help me, for fear that I might somehow endanger them. I would never want to cause them harm.

The story I am about to tell is most difficult. I must start at the beginning, but some of the details from all those many years ago are lost to me now, or they are hazy and difficult to bring to mind. I have lived a dozen lives in the past several years, and I am only now beginning to recollect where it all began.

3

Cultural anthropology is the study of people. When I tell people what I do for a living, when I describe my work to them, they most often tell me that I am an archaeologist just like Indiana Jones. I have enjoyed the Indiana Jones movies, even the one with the aliens, but Indiana Jones does not do the work of an archaeologist no matter how many times he may tell people that he is one. He is first and foremost an action movie star, though I suppose he could also reasonably be called a treasure hunter or a looter. Those are not nice words to use regarding someone so loved by the general population, but they more accurately describe the work he performs than does the word "archeologist."

Interestingly, I can understand how a person could be confused by the actual work that I do because some aspects of cultural anthropology are similar to some aspects of archeology. We both dig in the dirt for remnants of older, ancient peoples and civilizations, we both attempt to piece together the everyday lives and rituals of those people, and we both present as complete a picture as we can of those people to better understand our own human development and evolution. Probably one of the biggest differences between the work of an archeologist and my work as a cultural anthropologist would be the ages of the people groups that we study, because I am dealing with the study of people who lived within the last few thousand years while my archeologist colleagues are digging far deeper into the earth as they are studying those people, those pre- and early humans, who lived some millions of years ago. The prehistoric people.

I first became aware of this particular site when a colleague of mine in Germany sent me a copy of an article published in *Der Spiegel* more than 30 years before which mentioned a Romanian family's attempt to relocate deeper into the forest but were stopped by members of the Romanian government because of a prior lease on the land by the Orthodox Church of the region. That lease made mention of a structure on the property that was said to have been in use by the church for nearly 2,000 years, which is an amazing piece of information. It seemed to be a bit of family folk- lore, a curious story spoken over the dining tables to entertain the guests, but though I dismissed it out-of-hand, the story remained with my waking moments for some months after. I have discov- ered in my years doing field research that many times a story such as that is the interesting angle from which a certain truth can be revealed. I won- dered if this might also be the same.

A graduate student of mine at the time, I will call him "Ron" to protect his identity, though I have no idea if he even still lives, began doing some research for me on this particular site and the lease in question and the claim being made by the Orthodox Church of the region. The World Wide Web is a wonderful, modern tool for just such endeavors, and his research uncovered many more interesting nuggets of information. The original article in *Der Spiegel* seemed to have had a couple errors in their reporting of the situation, most egregiously that it was not the Orthodox Church of the region that laid claim to the religious structure, but it was a splinter group, a Christian cult of some kind that had not actually been seen anywhere in Romania or Bulgaria, Hungary, Serbia, and not even as far north as Ukraine for more than 50 years at that time. People suspected the Soviet Union's military presence in Romania had done much to stifle their presence, either through an outright military campaign against the religious sect or simply by the Soviet military's brief presence and control of the country. Either way, the Orthodox Church made no such claim to the land or the structure as had been mentioned in the *Der Spiegel* article, the family members that had made the original petition to build deeper into the forest had all seemed to have died off, and the main property, the forest around that property, and that "original," old structure had all been claimed by the government as abandoned property.

Interestingly enough, when Ron contacted a colleague I had met from the University of Bucharest to request of her any more information she might have on the site, she became quite excited about our interest because she too had only recently heard rumors of a site of some importance in that same region of the country. Within only a few weeks she returned our enquiries with the most amazing report, that not only had she been to visit the site, but that she had seen for herself the structure that had been reported and that it looked to be of a type associated with many of the early Christian hidden churches that sprang up throughout the region during the Roman persecution of those Christians.

With so much excitement regarding this site, we immediately began making preparations to begin working together to explore and uncover as much information as we could on this hidden structure of the 1st-century persecuted Christian community. Unfortunately as with all things academic, we were delayed by funding requests and travel vouchers, even government permissions and requests for graduate assistants. It took Ron and me most of the rest of that year to make the arrangements we needed and to coordinate our travel plans with my Romanian colleague and to gather the remainder of our student workers and travel the 30+ hours to reach the other side of the world.

It is most unlikely that you will have heard of

anywhere we traveled within Romania, but for the sake of a complete record, I will share with you that we landed in Bulgaria where we met with my colleague and enjoyed a wonderful tour of her beautiful city. That was probably the last of our leisure and happy times. Next we traveled by van north in the country to Dornisoara, just off the Prislop River, where we took several back roads to reach the tiny hamlet of Mihai, just 15 km to the east. The students, of course, were excited by our proximity to the Calimani National Park and the opportunities to go skiing, but of course we had our work to complete. There would be time enough for the national park later.

We left Mihai and drove a dirt path as far as we could in the van, and then the hike from the road through the dense forest was long and tiring and uphill the entire way and far past the local tree line, but to finally see the site with our own eyes was amazing. Again, if you have seen the action films you likely have a preconceived idea of the site, such as an ornate cathedral in the heart of the forest or a city face hewn from the earth and stones. Unfortunately, real life is seldom as glamorous as Hollywood would make us to believe, but this site was a joy to behold in its own right. The earthen mounds stood out to us immediately, seven of them built up into a circle surrounding a central mound that looked to have been shaved off on one side, as if a piece had fallen away or possibly been cut away from it. We did not immediately recognize how prescient that first reaction would be.

That first day was spent measuring and squaring the site, setting up our grid lines and reviewing our preliminary data and analyses to begin working in the months ahead. We had been granted long-term, exclusive access to the property, and we were quite excited to begin as quickly as possible and see what we might uncover. I of course was most interested in that squared off section of the center earthen mound, the one that we found most unusual when we first arrived, and after much discussion with my Romanian colleague, we agreed that would be one of our first dig spots.

Removing the topmost soil levels was relatively quick, and we were soon finding many interesting items from the past few hundred years, evidence of fires on the site, evidence of people cooking and using the site for traveling, for sewing. As we dug deeper, the years sprang to life around us as we found utensils from the 1800s, a porcupine quill needle from the 1700s, and even a stenbrish (sic) that looked to come from the early 1600s. It was at that time, however, that the ground fell away beneath us, and I mean that quite literally. That hollowed out portion of earthen mound revealed a hole cut through a stone slab that led to a small tunnel deep into the earth. Not any ordinary, animal tunnel, mind, we would have known that for certain. This tunnel was most interesting because it had been carved by human tools and human hands, and it did, indeed, appear to be more than 1,500 years old.

4

The hole itself was quite narrow, but obviously chiseled to allow passage underground. We shone our lights into the hole and could see that a series of tunnels had been carved through it and reinforced with more rock slabs along the floor and against the walls. It was a most interesting find, quite unexpected but exciting. The passage was wide enough that only the largest man among us could not fit through, but even so we agreed to be cautious in our endeavors, and so I alone, being the smaller of the researchers, ventured down in with my headlamp and camera to begin an initial examination. Now people might be thinking of catacombs or tombs, as if from some Hollywood blockbuster, but the reality was nothing like that. It was a network of tunnels, quite ancient and likely used by early Christians to avoid persecution from the authorities. Of course I knew none of this at the time, I am merely stating now what I learned from our work soon after this discovery.

The tunnels were alternately shorter and taller such that I could almost stand to my full height in one, but I had to squat and do a sort of crab walk in the next, but then in one I was forced to lie flat and crawl through the dirt on my belly. At last I chose a well-worn path to follow, one in which the stone slabs upon the ground had been scuffed smooth by years of people stepping upon them, and I followed that path to see where it would lead. Etchings and writings adorned the rock slab walls, and I took pictures of so many of them, their images through the viewfinder still in my mind all these years later. So many intricate images, so much detail, and even some bits of ancient writing, both Latin and Greek and, of particular interest, even some lines of ancient Hebrew, just like the texts of the scrolls I am beginning to translate. It was truly remarkable, and such a great loss.

As wondrous as those rock walls were, however, the tiny room at the end of that tunnel was a treasure house, for that is the room where I first made the discovery of the scrolls. The walls were lined with stone shelves, and upon each shelf was laid out dozens of scrolls of varying sizes and lengths, many of which were written in different languages, and some of which contained interesting and exciting illustrations. The pieces I could immediately see already seemed almost too remarkable, too unbelievable to have been buried in this little underground chamber for nearly 2,000 years, but the proof was sitting on the shelves before me, unable to be denied.

I wished to disturb the documents as little as possible. As I've already said, I am not some real-life Indiana Jones, and I had no wish to destroy my valuable find by "rescuing it" from its millenniums-long home. I found one document, a small one that was sitting by itself, and I retrieved it from its alcove and secured it in a transport container, after taking numerous pictures and documenting its location and condition, of course. I do not wish you to think I was a sloppy researcher, so please know that we took extra care with all of the work we conducted in those underground passageways. Our meticulous efforts were not rewarded, as you shall soon read, but we did the work all the same.

Upon first opening the container and revealing

the artifact I retrieved from the underground library, my Romanian colleague became ecstatic with joy. All of our hard work was proving true, and we felt vindicated in our pursuit of this site. She was most especially interested in a colleague of her own seeing this particular find, a researcher she said would be able to help us. She said he was a monk at the Suceava Monastirea, just to the north of Dornisoara, who had made it his life's work to research early Christian artifacts, both the history of them and the authentication of them. This seemed fortuitous, that our site would be located so near to such an expert and at the same time we would uncover from our site just such an artifact that could be examined and possibly expounded upon by someone with exactly the knowledge we required, and if I had known then what I know now about this man's loyalties, I never would have agreed to allow him to view the scroll.

Though the distance was short, the drive itself was long because of the twisting back roads, first from our site along the Prislop, through Mihai, and then along the narrow road out of Dornisoara and out to the monastery itself. The monastery grounds were expansive, and they were filled with numerous buildings of mammoth stones and small windows and a wall of medium height that surrounded the entire complex and kept foot and auto traffic flowing in particular directions. There was a large, open gate through which we drove, a narrow road to a small parking lot, and a man of the cloth to greet us when we arrived. I made note of the circle-G carved above the door but did not then know its meaning or its significance, or I might then have insisted on us leaving.

The priest ushered us into a small library room filled floor to ceiling with theological, scientific, artistic, medicinal, and even botanical and herbological texts, both old and new, although several of which dated back to more than 100 years ago. We had little time to peruse those interesting texts, however, as The Right Reverend Archimandrite Edmundo Solis soon joined us. He was an impressive man who stood straight and tall and with a full head of the brightest white hair I have ever seen on an elderly man. He was most interested in the scroll when we revealed it to him, and he studied it with the care and delicacy of the finest research scientists with whom I have had the pleasure of working.

With his assistance, we were able to interpret several lines of the text, but his enthusiasm dimmed for the project with each completed word. The Right Reverend Archimandrite Edmundo Solis grew quite concerned that we might not be dealing with a genuine artifact but might instead have uncovered a well preserved but fraudulent creation. We assured him we would be looking into just such a possibility with great care, and that is when he offered his expert services on our behalf. As he was quite familiar with the language and had already claimed to have successfully translated several lines, he offered to complete the entire translation for us within a fortnight, or possibly even sooner. I was reluctant to leave behind such a potentially valuable piece of historical artifact, but my Romanian colleague assured me she had complete faith in his abilities and impeccable professionalism. I reluctantly agreed to the arrangement, and we returned to the site.

By the time we arrived back at the camp, it was rather late and quite dark. The students had already eaten, and several had turned in for the night. I was unaware at that time, however, that one of the students, a lovely young man named

Blake from Tennessee in the United States, had gone missing. Unfortunately, none of the other students was aware either, and we did not notify the local authorities until the following morning. He was never located.

5

———

Those regional authorities, a group of officers from far away, the police officer of Dornisoara, and a constable stationed in Mihai, interviewed the members of our team thoroughly, taking nearly the entire following day to meet with each of us in turn as well as in a group, and then we all assisted them in scouting the forest around our site. Even with the assistance of a team of trained scouting hounds, there was no indication of where Blake could have gone, except for his scent that was picked up by the hounds along the path back to the main road. At the time it seemed confusing to us all where he might have gone or how he might have left when my Romanian colleague and I had taken the only vehicle with us to the monastery, but as I think upon it now, I must wonder if he was not possibly somehow attracted from the camp and then spirited away by members of the same order who have so made my life difficult in the years since. I wish I could know the truth of his disappearance, but I fear I may never learn that.

It was the bulk of two days we spent being interviewed and assisting with the search, and then my Romanian colleague and I consoled and counseled our remaining and distraught graduate students. They were rightly concerned for their friend, but there was nothing we could do for him but allow the local authorities to do their job and to alert the universities to the lovely young man's disappearance. It was morning of the third day when we were finally able to resume our activities, though the pace was significantly slowed by the torpor that now resided in our graduate students.

We spent that day and the next several meticulously cataloging the scrolls and various artifacts within the chamber we had now begun referring to as "the library." This was probably the time of most productivity and calm and joy of all the days we spent on our site. It certainly felt the most academically invigorating to me, the most interesting time to be working in the field. It would not last, of course, but it was good nonetheless.

It was about six days after the disappearance of our graduate student, Blake, that The Right Reverend Archimandrite Edmundo Solis paid us a personal visit at the site. My Romanian colleague was most impressed that he would travel all that way to see us, though it did not seem all that far to me, and she insisted that we show him everything, which seemed against my better judgment at the time, but she assured me again he was a respected scholar throughout the region and that a simple tour could do no harm. We showed him the circle of mounds and the collapsed hole and the tunnel, though he could barely fit down through, and when we showed him the library, he became quite serious and grim. He shook his head, and I do not believe I will ever forget his mumbled words:

"Sadly, I am correct. All fakes and forgeries."

I knew he was incorrect. In my heart and in my head, I knew he was incorrect. The weeks we had spent digging, and the days we had spent cataloging and collecting these hundreds of scrolls and documents, the thousands of total hours that I and my Romanian colleague and our graduate students had spent analyzing and tallying and tagging and cataloging, and I knew that The Right Reverend Archimandrite Edmundo Solis's declaration was false.

An argument ensued, of course, and my Romanian colleague later castigated me for being rude to him, but I could not stand by silently as he so disparaged our hard work, the work of our students, and this most interesting find. I must admit, however, to being a bit overzealous in my boisterous defense of our work as I yelled at him and demanded that he leave. Interestingly, he would not be put off, and he yelled right back at me and made the most absurd claims about my education and pedigree, and he then began yelling at me in Spanish, which I happen also to know, and so I too switched languages, and that is when my Romanian colleague became most agitated and said we should continue our conversation at a later date, though I was not at all inclined to do that.

As we emerged from underground, several of the graduate students were gathered near the hole, for they had obviously heard the commotion. They stepped away immediately as our argument continued and we walked through the forest and on toward the Right Reverend's vehicle. I am somewhat embarrassed to say that by this time I had worked myself into a fair bit of anger, and I was defending our work loudly enough as to frighten the birds in the trees. The graduate students were hanging far back from us, possibly out of fear, possibly out of embarrassment, and my Romanian colleague had abandoned any attempt at reconciling us and also remained far back at the campsite.

That was when something most interesting transpired. The Right Reverend Archimandrite Edmundo Solis stopped arguing, stopped walking through the forest to his vehicle, and turned and simply stared at me. Of course I was confused. I had no idea what this change in behavior was meant to signify, and I faltered on my words and quickly came to a halt in my arguments. At that, he stared at the ground, clasped his hands behind his back, and advanced slowly toward me. I do not back down, and I did not then either, and it was almost immediate that he was in my personal space. He bent down a bit toward me, and he whispered this warning to me:

"I make this offer once. Leave now, or I cannot be responsible for what happens next."

I was stunned. He had actually threatened me.

I don't know how long I stood there staring at him. I probably had my mouth open wide, I was in such shock at what he had said to me. I do know, however, that it was long enough that he became amused and grinned at me. Yes, it was an actual grin. The bastard. And then he said something that is far more chilling now than I even realized it to be at the time:

"Understand, I cannot protect you. The Gnostic Brocade demands you abandon this site, or…." As his voice trailed off, his smiled vanished, and his look turned quite grave, as if he had just delivered notice of someone's death. Which, as I soon learned, was exactly what he had done.

6

I should have taken his words more seriously. I should have taken greater precautions. I allowed myself to believe his words were an empty threat, that nothing would really happen to our little group so deep in the forest. It is so simple to look back now and to see that the signs were all there, that if I had simply heeded that small voice inside me, the one that screamed, "Leave," several more people might still be alive. But I did not. And that is my burden to bear.

We wrapped our work early that day and gave the students several hours of free time and the use of our Rover to go into the village. They were subdued, almost as if they were afraid to speak, and I cannot say I blamed them. My Romanian colleague barely spoke to me the rest of the day, and so I used my time alone to surreptitiously move our artifacts to a more remote location within the forest. At the time I was unsure exactly why I felt I must do that, perhaps because of the words the Right Reverend had spoken to me, or perhaps it was some divine inspiration I felt called to heed. Whatever the reason, I worked alone throughout that afternoon meticulously checking our catalog, padding the artifacts, packing them securely in their transport crates, and securing them in a cut-out cave along the path to the road. I did not know at the time if anyone observed me make those preparations, but I am confident to say now that no one did.

I had a silent, emotionally-cold evening at supper with my Romanian colleague, and then we retired in more silence to our tents. The students returned late into the night; they attempted silence as they stumbled along the path, but it was clearly evident to me they had consumed large quantities of alcohol, and neither speaking quietly nor sneaking along the path came easily to them. In short order they were back inside their tents and sleeping soundly, and the quiet of the midnight forest returned. I slept fitfully. My thoughts and dreams were worried, scattered, and I was afraid.

It was my difficulty sleeping that allowed me to

hear the movement in the dark. It was footsteps, and many of them. I padded softly to the tent door and looked outside, but I could see nothing. Something within me told me to remain quiet as I slipped from my tent and snuck behind some trees. I could hear the soft movements, the rustle of fabrics and the occasional snaps of sticks. Within moments, however, the sounds were gone, and I felt I was once again alone in the woods.

I crept through the dark forest, carefully setting my feet so as not to make the same kinds of noises that had awakened me. I circled the camp that way once, then twice, but I heard nothing more and saw no one. I had given up, chided myself for being scared, or paranoid, and was just returning to my tent when I heard more noises, this time from the dig itself, and that is when the panic struck me. The footsteps had not gone away; they had gone underground. Into the heart of our site. Into the tunnels. Looters!

I turned and ran, this time not caring the noise I made, but it was already too late when I arrived. I caught the merest glimpses of shadows running off into the forest, but I also saw something much worse. It was not looters that had descended upon our camp. It was destroyers, pillagers, the ravagers of history. I could see the flickering glow through the small opening in the earth. They had set fire within the tunnels.

With no heed to my own safety, I yelled for assistance and ran for the tunnel entrance. Though I had covered the hole with a plastic tarp as I did every night, the defilers had sliced through that, and I saw smoke and flickering light coming through the hole and up from below the ground. I slid to the ground and wriggled my way through the narrow opening and dropped to the tunnel floor below. It was all bright and smoky, and I had the most trouble breathing that I have ever had in my life. I immediately started coughing, and I turned toward the direction of the library, now such habit that I knew instinctually which way to go, and I was heartbroken to see that the brightest fires came from that direction, from within the small library vestibule. I ran forward, but the fire and the heat made it impossible for me to approach, and all I could do was stand back and cough and watch the fires devour that treasure trove of documents.

I'm not sure how long I remained there, but the smoke choked out all breath, and I soon found myself collapsing to the floor as one of our interns gripped me from behind and pulled me away from the fire. He had a rope looped around his belly, and he tied another bit of it around me and helped me back to the tunnel entrance. By this time I could barely stand, and I fell several times, and the coughing would not stop. A pair of hands pulled me back up through the hole in the ground, and I collapsed in the frigid night air and watched as our intern was helped back up. Then I laid there on my side and watched the smoke pour through that hole and the flames beneath the earth flicker brighter with each passing moment. History was destroyed that night. A whole culture was obliterated from the face of the Earth, erased for all time because someone did not like what it had to say. Because someone was too insecure in his own beliefs to allow an alternative perspective to be brought forth into the full light of day and the scrutiny of the worldwide research community. All because of jealousy, or ignorance. Or perceived blasphemy. I have never hated the gods of this world more than I hated them all that night as I watched all of that knowledge vanish forever.

7

The fire could not be put out. As I learned much later, the despicable men who did it had used an accelerant, likely petrol, though the police did not clarify, and they splashed it upon every bit of combustible material beneath the earth. My Romanian colleague rushed me into Dornisoara as quickly as she could along the rough mountain road. The nearest medical of any kind, Dispensary Medical Bistrita Bargaului, was over 50 km away, and so we went straight to the police, which turned out to be nothing more than a territorial unit stationed in the town, and it was closed. The next nearest was 70 km away.

Once we awakened the officer, he sat me at a small, wooden desk and made me wait as he organized his notes and prepared the paperwork to process my complaint. I sat quietly in my chair, though I had trouble breathing, and my arms and

knees were scraped and bleeding. I coughed con-
stantly, even after the officer glared at me as he
poured his coffee. When he finally allowed me to
tell my story, he sat and drank his coffee and lis-
tened, but he took no notes, and then he requested
I repeat my story. And again, though he finally
took notes the third time I told it. He interviewed
my Romanian colleague in a separate room, and
then he interviewed me again. It was wearisome,
and my body ached both inside and out from the
coughing, though the bleeding on my arms and
legs finally stopped and my bruises purpled.

He reviewed my paperwork, including my
passport and university credentials and all of the
receipts and boarding passes I had kept from my
flight into the country. He made me wait in that
hard chair as he went to another room, and I heard
him making phone calls to God knows who, people in different countries as he fought with the
old landline and yelled into the receiver, as if the
people in those other countries would understand
him better if he was louder. I know he contacted
my university, and he was quite aggrieved that he
could get no one to speak with him about my work
presence, which is not surprising as my university

was on the other side of the world and everyone had likely gone home for the day. He spoke much quieter on another set of calls, and I felt as if he was speaking to his superiors. There were many affirmatives and much listening on those calls. And finally he made one more call that I am now quite certain was made to a member of the Gnostic Brocade, that secretive organization of which I have already written several times. His voice was quite quiet, and once he even set down the receiver and checked on me that I was still in my chair, and then he shut the door and returned to his call.

By this time I had been sitting in that chair for several hours. The sun was well up, and the people outside were going about their daily business. My Romanian colleague had been dismissed following her interview, and I never saw her again, not back at the site, and not ever again while I was escaping her country. I like to think that she returned to her university and resumed her own research, but she has returned none of my telephone calls or emails in the intervening years, and I fear for her safety. She may be watched or under guard, or she may be simply keeping her distance from me as a precaution against drawing any further unwanted attention, which is the reason I have so diligently refrained from naming her here. If she ever reads this document, I wish her all the best in this life and in the next. We had our differences, but I valued our friendship, and we had a delightful comradery for such a long time. I miss those years.

It was about this time that the police officer stepped back into his office and looked at the security camera mounted near the ceiling and then looked back at me and said I was free to leave. He could determine that I had committed no crime, and he found no reason to hold me any longer. I began to protest, of course, that it was not I who had committed a crime, but it was those men who invaded our campsite in the middle of the night, but he merely held up his hand and repeated again and again that as I had committed no crime I was free to leave. He insisted that I get up from the hard chair, and he escorted me to the front door, telling me the entire time that I was lucky to be found innocent and that I was free to leave, though when I requested the return of my paperwork, he declined, telling me that my paperwork was being reviewed and that a ranking officer would be visiting me at the site in the very near future to let me know if everything had been approved or not.

I argued with him all the way out to the sidewalk, and that is when he grew grave. He leaned forward and whispered into my ear that I must leave immediately, that I must gather my belongings and flee the country as quickly as possible, that I must leave before the ranking officer drove up from the station and went to the site. When I protested that I needed my paperwork to leave the country, he shook his head and whispered, "The Gnostic Brocade has it. There is nothing I can do for you but give you this warning. Leave now. Quickly."

With that, he pushed me outside and slammed the door shut.

8

I walked through town and thumbed a ride. A kindly man drove me as far as the crossroads. It was cold that morning, and I had not been thinking clearly enough after the fire to bring along my overcoat, so the walk was slow and miserable. My leg ached where I had fallen through the hole, and it hurt to take deep breaths. I most likely should have been seen by a doctor, but I was not sure how much time I had left following the policeman's warning to leave the area. Hiking through the forest in my condition was exhausting, and it seemed to take me hours to get back to the campsite, and when I finally did so I found it destroyed. The tents had been burned down, our supplies had been gutted and scattered, and worst of all, our students were gone. At the time I was distraught for their safety, but I learned much later that they had been sent home. Their personal effects were confiscated, but the students themselves were un-harmed. (If you are reading this now, my wonderful graduate students, know that I am so very sorry for what happened. If I could take it all back now and keep you from any harm, I certainly would do so.)

I found the hole to the underground chamber easily enough because a thin line of smoke still drifted out of it and up into the sky. As I approached, the air got hotter and hotter. Heat was drifting up from the ground beneath my feet. The heat hurt my face as I leaned over to peer inside the hole, but I had to know what had been done, though my suspicions were confirmed. The entire underground site had been filled with piles of steaming, hot, glowing rocks. It was raw coal that had been dumped underground and piled around and then lit on fire. In some spots it was so hot that the earthen walls seemed actually to be glowing. The sight of all that destruction began to make me sick to my stomach, or perhaps it was the additional smoke and fumes I was breathing in, but I had to get away from there as quickly as I could.

I stumbled through the forest for a while after

that, too much in agony at everything I had witnessed and been a part of, however unwilling my part in the destruction had been. Somewhere in the back of my mind I continued hearing the police officer tell me I had to get away, and that I had to do it quickly, but I was so distraught that I could hardly think correctly. When I finally realized what I was doing, the sun was much higher in the sky, and I began to panic that I had wasted too much time.

The cases were just to the east of our campsite, and I prayed that they had been untouched as I ran through the woods to reach them. The small cave was damp, and the sun did not penetrate very deeply into the cave, but my cases were still there and still in a safe condition. I would not be able to carry them as they were, with all of the protective padding required of transporting documents of such value back to my research lab at the university, but I knew I could not risk leaving any of them behind. (I had seen what my foes were capable of doing to such important documents.) And so I quickly set about unpacking the cases, removing the protective paddings, and stashing these valuable documents in a much lighter, more easily transported carrying case. I knew I was sac-rificing durability in favor of size and portability, but at that point I simply had little choice. I had to flee, and I could not leave these remaining docu-ments to be destroyed.

It was a long, arduous trek back out of the for-est, and by the time I made it back out to the main road and thumbed another ride, this time from a passing truck, I could just see the flashing lights of more police as they headed out to our destroyed site, most likely to arrest me on some trumped-up charge.

9

As I sit here today I can only ponder the great changes that have come into my life over the past several years. Once I had a career. Once I had friends and family. Once I had a life. But no more. I have been in hiding throughout various parts of the United States. At times I am homeless. At times I have been running from various people who have tried to harm me or to steal my materials. I am so very fortunate as to write now that I have not lost a single document that came with me out of Romania, though I have come very close at least several times, most especially once in London, England, and another time in Amarillo, United States.

My vision is no longer what it was many years ago, and I find it more difficult to compose my thoughts on the computer now that I am missing the smallest finger on my left hand, although the speech recognition software is absolutely marvelous for this amount of dictation, limited though it is. These hardships are worth the expense paid, however, so that I may bring this knowledge into the world, no matter the resistance I encounter.

It is most interesting to me that these documents I and my colleagues uncovered in Romania should warrant such intent interest by a group such as the Gnostic Brocade. As I have studied and perused the scrolls, which I have now taken to calling the Dornisoara Scrolls, these several years, I have found much to fascinate me and that I believe should be shared, but little that should generate such hostility. By all appearances the documents contain secret knowledge from 2,000 years ago, but no more secret than that knowledge contained within the Dead Sea scrolls or most especially the Nag Hammadi texts uncovered in the last century, yet there was no such extreme reaction from anyone when those discoveries were made. The texts are unique, and they provide a different perspective on the events of 2,000 years ago, certainly, but I find nothing of such scandalous importance that it should not be revealed to all. It in some ways feels reminiscent of the protests and outcries related to the desecration of native sites, such as was done when a Native American burial site in Cannonball, North Dakota, United States, was bulldozed to make passageway for a gas pipeline. Unlike that incident, however, my Romanian colleague and I found no evidence of any indigenous population living in that part of the country, and other than the cryptic warnings from the Right Reverend Archimandrite Edmundo Solis as well as vague comments from the police officer of Dornisoara that my safety might be in jeopardy, we received no proper notification that our presence was unwelcome or that our research was in any way offensive to any indigenous group. Even if that were to be true, however, that some indigenous group was to be found living in that region, the wholesale destruction of the site simply for the sake of keeping knowledge such as this a secret from the world would be unethical. Who would do such a thing? Destroyers and looters, certainly.

No, my duty now, my burden for me to carry, is to bring these documents to the world, no matter the resistance I encounter. I have been forced to remain hidden from the world, conducting my translation work and research and commentary writing in secret, late at night and in the lowliest of places. I have found myself hidden in the center of large cities as well as the most remote villages and farmlands as I have sought to keep myself safe from the scrutiny of those who would do me harm. I recently spent a most interesting year of relative serenity along the outskirts of the Williston man-camps of North Dakota, observing the oil boom from up close, finding work where I could to supply me with rice and beans, and feeling nostalgia for the days of my youth on these mid-American prairies. I have moved on, of course, but the time there was good for my soul.

I write this information for you, dear reader, as well as for my friend, H. Dean Fisher, as a record of my time and my efforts and my passion. You must know what I know. You must see the importance of these scrolls and this history. You must not let this knowledge fade away. I wish all God's blessings upon you.

2

The Revelation of Simon, Son of Cuphythis

10

The Revelation of Simon
Chapter 1

1. The revelation of Simon, Son of Cuphythis, given to him as a gift of Jesus, the Nazarene, given to Him by God Almighty, the Father, the One who is and was and is to come.

2. He made it known what could be endured and the punishment that would be received, and sent his revelation through an angel to his servant Simon, who testifies truthfully of everything that he saw and heard.

3. May the one who comes after this servant be blessed by the words of this testimony, and may his life receive the fullness of the measure of true blessings that are to come; and may a thousand millstones tether to purgatory the one who alters

the meaning of these words so that no reward may ever be received except that which shall also be granted the Witness. Amen.

4. Be sure in your faith, for the time is near.

5. I, Simon, your brother and fellow traveler in the Way, was lost with a downcast heart at the Desolation we witnessed on Mt. Sinai.

6. The Lord let loose His wrath at the stubborn and wicked generation, striking down the ones who committed adultery with the Golden Calf.

7. They were blinded and could not seek out the serpent to cleanse them from their wickedness and unrighteousness.

8. They were swallowed whole by the Earth, never again to find solace at the feet of the Lord our God.

9. It was with crushing vindication that the Lord wiped away the memories of their hard hearts, of the disloyalty they showed to Him all the short days of His time with us.

10. It was on that day that I, Simon, went forth into the desert to seek His face.

11. I journeyed thirty-nine days, neither eating

nor drinking, but crying out to the Lord for mercy, and it was on that fortieth day that He heard His servant's cry and answered, "Who is that seeking the Lord?"

12. "It is I," I answered, "Simon, son of Cuphythis, servant of the Lord Jesus who is the Christ."

13. The Lord replied, "I Am," and the earth became as silent as the hour before creation.

14. I turned to see the voice that was speaking, but fell face down at the feet of the Lord our God.
15. His head glowed with the glory of the noonday sun, His hands and feet were like bronze, and His eyes blazed with the righteousness of the One who came before.

16. I cried out, "Lord, your servant is not worthy to stand in Your presence. Please send another."

17. But the Lord replied, "I have sent whom I have sent," and the world became night. The first sign.

11

<hr>

The Revelation of Simon
Chapter 2

1. It was in that desolate stillness that I heard a cry echo into the void.

2. It was a cry of pain and anguish, the cry of one who is lost and cannot find solace, a cry of one wandering in the wilderness.

3. I looked up to see who had cried out to the Lord, and I found myself standing in the Tabernacle, His Holy Dwelling Place in the desert.

4. Around me stood four men who looked to be Sons of God.

5. They were dressed in gold breastplates, with blue sashes across their chests.

6. Their helmets glowed, and the laces of their shoes seemed to pulse with the light of the Living

God.

7. They stood one at each wall of the Tabernacle, their swords in hand and guarding the curtains that opened into the sacred rooms.

8. The One to the West stood with his sword buried in the sand; the One to the North held his sword straight toward me; and the One to the East held his sword high above his head, his lips parted in prayer to the Almighty; at the south entrance stood the final One, his sword held loose at his side as he watched the other three, his eyes continually moving from west to east and back again.

9. The One to the South spoke, saying, "Who is it who calls into the wilderness? Who cries out for the Lord to save him?"

10. "It is I," replied the One to the North.

11. He pressed the point of his sword to my chest, and I felt the burning heat tear into my flesh as the Word of the Lord pierced my soul.

12. Then the One to the North turned, parted his curtain, and stepped through his door.

13. At his beckoning, I followed.

14. The desert fell away at my feet, and I was left walking through what had once been the Jordan River.

15. It was now a dry bed, parched and cracking in the heat of the noonday sun.

16. Bones were scattered all around, the bones of the witnesses and the shards of the twelve lampstands.

17. The earth shook as a mighty wind pounded the bones and the shards with the force of a thousand storms, lightning leaping into the sky, and the heavens clapping with the joy of righteousness.

18. The One who walked before me continued on as a second wind pounded the earth, the bones and the shards jumping into the air and falling back again.

19. At the third strike of the wind, the air grew still, and the bones floated as dust to the ground.

20. The shards of the twelve lampstands had become as a million tongues of flame scattered throughout the river bed.

21. Then the One to the North stopped and turned toward me.

22. "Son of man, can these flames quench the mouths of the dry and thirsty bones?"

23. I said, "My Lord, you alone know."

24. Then he said to me, "Prophesy to these bones and say to them, 'Dry bones, hear the word of the Lord. This is what the Sovereign Lord says to these bones: I will make the tongues of flames enter you, and you shall receive life like you have never before known.

25. I have gathered you on the third morning's light, I have gathered you and ground you in a hand mill and crushed you in a mortar.

26. You shall be cooked with the light of the new dawn's flame, and you shall be formed into loaves.

27. You shall taste like something made of olive oil, and you shall quench the thirst of this dry and parched land.

28. Then the world shall know that I am the Lord your God."

29. So I prophesied as the Lord had commanded, and the bones began to rattle and glow.

30. They grew together into a great body with the

heads and hands and legs of everyone now joined as one, and the million flames of the shards of the lampstands set the great body on fire, and its flames filled the riverbed of the Jordan River.

31. Then the One to the North turned and pointed to the end of the Jordan River, and there I saw the First Man standing in the desert and watching.

32. His body was wrapped in the bandages of the leper, the shepherd's staff at his side and the flies swarming around him.

33. His eyes looked into my soul, and I felt the despair of his affliction. Winter's death beckoned at his heel, but he would not approach the One to the North or the Great Body that now glowed in the Jordan River bed. He turned and walked away, spreading pestilence as he went.

34. The second sign.

12

———

The Revelation of Simon
Chapter 3

1. Immediately I was returned to the Tabernacle of the Lord, and the One to the North removed
the sword of the Word of the Lord from my chest.
2. The place burned where it left my soul, and I
flung myself to the ground in grief.
3. I cried out to the Lord that I might bear it a
while longer, but the One to the North sheathed
his sword and bowed his head.

4. The One to the South spoke then, saying, "Who
is it who calls into the wilderness?
5. Who cries out for the Lord to save him?"

6. "It is I," replied the One to the West, the One

like a Son of God who had buried his sword deep into the earth.

7. He pulled the sword free and placed the point of it to my head, and I felt the burning heat tear into my flesh as the Word of the Lord pierced my body.

8. Then the One to the West turned, parted his curtain, and stepped through his door.

9. At his beckoning, I followed.

10. The desert fell away at my feet, and I stepped into paradise.

11. The River of Life flowed beneath the feet of the angels of the Lord as they guarded the entrance, their swords swinging far and wide.

12. The One to the West stood at my side, watching and waiting.

13. Animals passed us by as they stepped beneath the feet of the angels and entered into paradise, pairs of each kind of animal returning to the good of creation.

14. Then the serpent passed me by, beckoning me to follow as it went.

15. I stamped my heel upon its head, but a second serpent followed the first.

16. I stamped my heel upon its head also, but a

third serpent followed the second.

17. I stamped my heel upon its head, and then looked to the face of the One to the West.

18. He wept as he looked upon the dying serpent.

19. "Forgive me," I pleaded, but the One would not hear my cry.

20. I ran forward in grief beneath the feet of the angels of the Lord, and as I entered into paradise, I called out to the Lord, "Forgive me."

21. The serpent passed me by once again, beckoning me forward.

22. This time I followed.

23. He led me past every pair of animals within the garden, and they all watched us go.

24. They turned their eyes away with tears at our passage, but they did not stretch out their arms to stop us.

25. The serpent led me past the Tree of the Knowledge of Good and Evil, and I bore witness to the destruction of its branch, the one from which the fruit had been removed.

26. The serpent led me past the Tree of Life, the one from which the fruit of the everlasting still re-

mained.

27. But the fruit had grown rotten upon the vine, and the serpent wept.

28. Then I heard a voice like the silken river call out upon the garden, "Come," and the serpent and I continued on.

29. We approached a mountain upon which sat the throne of the Lord, but it was empty.

30. The serpent went to the throne and sat beneath it and bowed.

31. I did the same.

32. Then the voice of the Lord echoed from the place of the throne, "Well done, my good and faithful servant."

33. I lifted my head to cry out to the Lord, but the serpent's voice already filled the void, and it praised the Lord on high.

34. When I turned away from the throne of the Lord, the First Man stood at my back.

35. He wore the withered garments of the leper, but they were filled with the stench of utter death.

36. His eyes were empty as he gazed into my being.

37. He wrapped his arms about me and spoke with

the voice of one who had died long before, and he said, "This is my witness. Proclaim it to the nations."

38. He turned and walked away, pestilence and disease spreading like a wake as he departed.
39. The third sign.

The Revelation of Simon
Chapter 4

1. Immediately I was returned to the Tabernacle of the Lord, and the One to the West removed the sword of the Word of the Lord from my head.
2. Tears welled within my soul, and I flung myself to the ground and wept.
3. I cried out to the Lord that I could not bear the weight of the witness, but the One to the West stood ready to plunge the sword back within me.

4. The One to the South spoke then, saying, "Who is it who calls into the wilderness?
5. Who cries out for the Lord to save him?"

6. "It is I," replied the One to the East, the One like

a Son of God who held his sword outstretched to the sky and moved his mouth in prayer.

7. I felt the longing within my soul, and I reached for the sword, to grasp its hilt and let its power shine within me.

8. The One to the East proclaimed, "Lord, my Lord, oh Lord, truly you are magnificent to bless the humble generations, the ones who see the mighty works of Your hand, who praise Your Holy Name, who receive mercy from generation unto generation."

9. Immediately we were cast through the curtain behind the One to the East, and we stepped upon a frozen shore.

10. The clouds hung as stars of ice upon the sky, the waves glittered in frozen ecstasy, and the air froze the breaths within my body.

11. Nothing moved, and the shore was silent.

12. "What is this place?" I asked.

13. The One to the East replied, "The strength of His will has shattered the hearts of the wicked.

14. He has brought down the mighty from their

thrones, and He has exalted the lowest among them."

15. I stepped forward and saw within the frozen waves that all living things moved within the waters, from the fish of the sea to the birds of the air to the men upon the ground – they all flowed through the living waters.

16. As I stepped again, the frozen waves parted so that I would not defile them with my touch, but they revealed the life within.

17. The animals and the people who had been within the waves stood all around and watched me pass upon the dry ground.

18. Some stood to the left, some to the right.

19. They all watched me pass as the frozen waves parted before me.

20. Those to the left cried tears of the fallen, their heads hung low and their bodies shaking in silent grief.

21. Those to the right cried out in silent praise, their arms uplifted to the heavens and their praises rising as wind upon the shore.

22. I walked upon that dry ground between the parting seas, never coming to its end for forty days

and forty nights.

23. Those upon my left grew more numerous, and those upon my right dwindled until they were almost no more.

24. The silent anguish of the condemned upon my left rang out within my soul, and as I felt I must stumble before its mighty weight, I cast my gaze upon the end of time.

25. The parting seas simply stopped.

26. The people upon my left and my right faded away.

27. The starlight shone from the ground around me, their lights more numerous than the stars upon the heavens.

28. There, upon that shoreline of stars, I cast my eyes once more upon the First Man.

29. He no longer wore the robes of the leper.

30. His flesh had been renewed.

31. Upon his brow was laid the crown of glory, and upon his fingers he bore the 12 rings of the tribes of Israel.

32. His face shown with the glory of the Lord, and he raised his arms in a blessing upon me.

33. At this, I fell face down before Him, and I praised His Holy Name, the first and the last.

34. He said, "Arise, and see what is to come.
35. Behold what tides of blessings and curses I shall cast upon the Earth before the end of all things."

36. I lifted my head from the sand to see what I might see of this revelation, but I found myself returned to the Tabernacle of the Lord.
37. The One to the East remained standing with his sword held high and his mouth uttering the praises of the Lord.
38. The fourth sign.

14

The Revelation of Simon
Chapter 5

1. The Tabernacle of the Lord remained silent as the ones like a Son of God stood to the East, the North, and the West.

2. The one to the South, however, was no longer there watching, and his curtain had been torn asunder.

3. A red robe and red sandals lay scattered upon the ground before that door.

4. "Put on the clothes of the righteous," spoke a voice from beyond the open door, "for you shall tread upon holy ground."

5. Immediately, I exchanged my stained and filthy

garments for the robe and sandals of red that lay upon the ground.

6. I peered into the open door, but saw only darkness.

7. I knew that I must enter, but I cried out in fear.

8. Receiving no reply, I prayed the Lord's protection and then stepped into the void, and my feet settled on the mountains of the Lord.

9. The first snows tore harshly at my body as I stumbled upon the path.

10. The wind howled its fury.

11. I looked out from the path and saw the world around me, from the Holy Mountain to the Desolate City.

12. Each step took me further upon the land, crossing rivers and

(DAMAGED TEXT – LARGE SECTION)

22. all the while moving through the blinding darkness, the blowing wind, and the rushing snow.

23. After a time, the Lord revealed to me the path on which I had been walking the entire time.

24. It was a well-worn path, wide through the mountains of the earth and bordered on one side by His Holy Temple and on the other by eternal torment.

25. The path was straight through the snowy night, but even though many had walked this way before, I walked the path alone this night – but I heard the faint cries of children.

26. I stepped to the right, toward the endless darkness, and I saw there upon the ground the bodies of the infants of the souls who had given themselves over to the Prince of that Darkness.

27. They sang an eternal psalm of mourning for the parents who had abandoned them upon the wide road, their voices a harmonious discord in the snowy night.

28. I stretched out my hand to lift them from out of their misery,

(DAMAGED TEXT – LARGE SECTION)

38. had given themselves over to the Prince of Peace.

39. They sang an eternal psalm of mourning also,

but theirs was for the parents who had taken them along upon the wide road only to see them through to their final resting place.

40. I reached out my hand to these infants also, to soothe their eternal cries, but at the sight of my aid, the infants turned their heads away.

41. Upon the backs of their necks rested the mark of the sacrifice of the Passover lamb.

42. At this, I called out to the Lord for guidance, but I received none.

43. The only voice I heard was the eternal night and the blowing snow and the cries of the infants, and so I continued on.

44. The path narrowed as I continued, the eternal darkness upon my right edging ever closer to the Temple of the Lord upon my left.

45. The singing stopped.

46. The wind stopped.

47. The snow stopped.

48. And I was left in the eternal stillness of that blackened night upon the path.

49. As I walked on, I soon came upon a small camp that looked to have been abandoned except the fire was still warm upon the ground.

50. A cooking pot rested on the ground beside the abandoned fire, a sword to the left of the pot and a cooking spoon to the right.

51. I knew within my heart that this was the camp of the witch of Endor.

52. Though I could not see her in that eternal darkness, I knew her to be watching me

(DAMAGED TEXT – SMALL SECTION)

57. He did not hear my cry.

58. At that moment, I reached the path's end.

59. The ground fell away before my feet, and the darkness swallowed it whole.

60. I looked around to see if that ended my journey, and I knew within my heart what it was the Lord had called upon me to do, that I was to cast aside the holy garments that had protected me this whole way.

61. I cried out to the Lord that I could not do that, that it would be blasphemy to cast them aside, but

62. He spoke within my heart again that I was to cast them aside.

63. And so I stripped naked at the end of that path and cast the tattered and holy garments of red into the abyss.

64. When I turned back to the path, the witch of Endor stood over her cooking pot, stirring her evening meal and watching me.

65. She beckoned me to return to her, but I was afraid.

66. I turned away and saw the Lord's Holy Temple standing where before there had been only darkness.

67. The Son of Man stood at the Temple

(DAMAGED TEXT – VERY SMALL SECTION)

69. with His warm embrace.

70. "You are worthy," He spoke, and I cried as he wrapped me in holy garments.

15

The Revelation of Simon
Chapter 6

1. The Son

(DAMAGED TEXT – VERY SMALL SECTION)

3. I looked and saw pairs of animals everywhere within this Temple, and I drew back in fear, for some there within were unclean.
4. The Son of Man walked through this Temple

(DAMAGED TEXT – VERY SMALL SECTION)

6. I followed at a distance, uncertain why the animals were allowed to defile the Temple.

7. Another man stood at the end of the Temple, the Witness of the Lord.

(DAMAGED TEXT – VERY SMALL SECTION)

9. He bore witness to the animals defiling the Holy Temple, to the Son of Man walking through, and to me following behind.

10. He bore witness to the cedars of Lebanon that had been carved within this Temple – the very temple King Solomon had constructed those years ago.

11. He bore witness to the golden lampstands at the Temple walls and the gold bowls and utensils sitting on the table of the Lord.

12. He bore witness to the Ark of the Covenant in its place at the front of the Temple, and he bore witness as the Son of Man lifted the lid off of the Ark, removed from it the Law and the Prophets, and unsealed them.

13. A great stillness settled over the Temple as all the pairs of animals of the earth waited.

14. All the animals except for a single raven that flew back and forth through the Temple, for it

could find no place to land within.

15. Outside, I heard the thunder roar, and I heard the great waters batter the Temple walls.

16. The purifying water rushed to and fro as the storm rolled outside, the storm of the judgment of the Lord upon all the peoples of the earth.

17. The Son of Man opened the Law and the Prophets He had removed from the Ark of the Covenant, and He read them aloud – but they were no longer the Law or the Prophets of old, for this Law and these Prophets had been transformed by His Holy presence.

18. He read, "The Lord sent a message against Jacob, and all of Israel knew it.

19. The bricks fell down, and were rebuilt with river stones.

20. The ash were cut down, but were replaced with the glorious cedars of Lebanon.

21. You went down to the king of Judah, and you proclaimed your message in his presence.

22. You said for him to do what was right, and he did what was right before the sight of the Lord.

(DAMAGED TEXT – LARGE SECTION)

32. which I commanded him at Horeb.

33. You beheld the return of Elijah the prophet before the coming of the great and terrible day of the Lord.

34. Your hearts were restored to your fathers, your fathers' hearts were restored to their children.

35. I, the Lord, held back My mighty hand and did not smite the land with a curse.

36. For those who mourned, the Lord gave comfort.

37. For those who were hungry or thirsty, the Lord gave food and drink.

38. For those who were peacemakers, they were called the children of God.

39. For those who were meek, they were given an inheritance in the Kingdom of God.

40. And for those who were pure in heart, the Lord showed His mighty face to them.

41. Thus did the Lord speak."

42. The Son of Man rolled the scroll and presented it to the Witness of the Lord who stood with his eyes covered by his holy garments.

43. At that, the single raven that had been flying back and forth within the Temple flew down and landed at the feet of the Son of Man.

44. It dropped a freshly plucked olive leaf at the feet of the Son of Man who raised His hands

(DAMAGED TEXT – LARGE SECTION)

54. a day's journey, the Witness stopped along the path, opened the Law and the Prophets given him by the Son of Man, and shook out the words of the Lord upon the ground before walking on.

55. As I passed that spot, I read the words that lay there, but they were not the words of the Lord as spoken in the Temple.

56. I followed again, and again he walked a day's journey down the mountain before stopping.

57. He opened the Law and the Prophets, and he shook out the words of the Lord upon the ground once again, but again the words that fell upon the ground were not the words the Lord had spoken.

58. I called out to the Witness, to tell him he was wrong, but he had already gone on.

59. He walked on like that, for seven days walking,

stopping, spilling the words of the Lord that were not the words of the Lord, then walking on again.

60. When we reached the base of the mountain, the people of the Lord were spread out before us, 12,000 from each of the tribes of Israel, 144,000 total, stood waiting to receive the words of the Lord, plus the gentiles that the Lord himself taught us to love.

61. They stood craving to receive the words of the Lord, and the Witness opened his book and shook them out upon the ground.

62. Where the words fell upon the ground, they took root, sprouted, and grew to be the largest fig trees of the desert, and the people of the Lord feasted upon the harvests that fell beneath those trees.

63. The fruit turned to ash in the mouths of the people, and they began retching where they stood.

64. I ran to the people of the Lord and told them of the corruption that had occurred, how the words of the Lord were not the words of the Lord, but they only laughed.

65. Then they filled their cloaks with the fruit

upon the ground and took it with them as they spread across every corner of the earth.

66. I looked out across

(DAMAGED TEXT – VERY SMALL SECTION)

68. and he blessed me where I stood.
69. Then he turned and continued on, the corrupted words of the Lord spilling from the Law and the Prophets that he carried with him as he went.

16

The Revelation of Simon
Chapter 7

1. I fell to the ground and cried out to the Lord.
2. I called out for Him to save us, to wipe away the corruption.
3. As I lay prostrate upon the ground, the First Man came and stood at my side.
4. His bandages were wrapped tightly about his body, but the blood spread upon them where the leprosy was taking hold.
5. The smell of death was upon him, and the flies circled him where he stood.
6. He turned his bandaged head toward me, and I saw the despair in his own eyes that matched my own.
7. I stood as the wind began to blow around us, a

powerful wind that the Lord sent upon us in that wooded desert.

8. It blew the sand up from the ground, a roaring wind that pounded the sand against our bodies, though it felt no worse than a gentle breeze.

9. The fig trees about us were torn up by their roots at the raging wind, and they blew across the desert like sticks.

10. Within moments, they were blown to the edge of the world and lost for all eternity.

11. Then the wind began to dig up the sand all around us.

12. It dug channels to the four corners of the world, driving out the sand from the desert.

13. As the sand was blown away, the Temple of the Lord began to be revealed before us, dug up by the wind.

14. The Temple walls, the courtyards, all were revealed as the sand was blown away.

15. I was about to rejoice at the Temple's resurrection, but the wind began to loosen the stones of the temple, to send them to the ends of the earth with the sand and the fig trees.

16. The walls were blown down, the Inner Sanc-

tums exposed, the Holy of Holies laid bare and the Ark of the Covenant tossed about by the blinding wind.

17. As I watched, a figure began to be revealed standing where before it had been the Ark in its holy place.
18. I first thought it to be one like the Son of Man, but it was the Witness again.
19. He stood where the Ark had rested, still holding the scrolls of the Law and the Prophets, and he tore them and sent them flying on the wind.
20. After each scroll he destroyed, he reached down to the place where the Ark had rested and pulled out another, then another.
21. The sand tore at the Witness' robes, but he took no heed, so intent was he upon the destruction of the Lord's word.

22. I tore at my robes and cried out for the Lord to stop this blasphemy, and then a sound like that of a hundred trumpets resounded throughout the desert and all became as black as night.

17

The Revelation of Simon
Chapter 8

1. The darkness surrounded me, and the world grew still.

2. The wind stopped.

3. The sand settled as dust upon the ground.

4. I stood alone and silent in that darkness for an age before I called out to the Lord, but He did not answer.

5. I began to walk, unsure where to go or what lay before me, but within moments I saw a light on the horizon.

6. It was faded, but it was steady, and I walked toward it.

7. As I traveled I came upon a blind man sitting upon the ground.

8. In one hand he held a fragment of the Law and the Prophets that had been torn and scattered upon the desert.

9. In his other hand he held a quill, and he was copying the scroll.

10. I reached forward to take the corrupted fragment from his hand, but before I could do that, I saw a second blind man not far off.

11. He too held a fragment, a different piece of the Law and Prophets that had been corrupted, and he too was copying it.

12. As I looked about, I saw more of these blind beggars sitting upon the ground, hurriedly copying the scraps of text they held.

13. "No!" I yelled out, and I ran through the desert night from one blind beggar to the next, trying to shake each from his stupor, but to no avail.

14. Then I called out to the Son of Man, cried out for Him to save me, and the blind beggars inclined their ears at my words.

15. "Listen," I cried out to them.

16. "Listen to the words of my lips, the words that have been given to me by the Son of Man. Listen to the message He has granted me, a message of

hope and a message of deliverance.

17. You need not remain in your stupor.

18. The Lord God of Israel, the God of our fathers, the God of Abraham and of Isaac and of Jacob, the One True God has spoken the truth to you.

19. His covenant He made with the children of Israel when we wandered in the desert.

20. He promised he would deliver us as He delivered us from out of Egypt.

21. He promised us manna and water in the desert, and He delivered.

22. We drank of the water that flowed from the rock, the water that the Lord promised and delivered so that even when Moses disobeyed and angered the Lord our God, He was still faithful and delivered.

23. "When the children of Israel asked for a king, He delivered and brought about the kingdom of David.

24. And even when King David disobeyed the Lord our God and had relations with Bathsheba, the Lord God remained faithful to the children of Israel, redeeming them from the wicked and the oppressors who stood at every side.

25. And the Lord our God rescued his servant David even from wickedness within his own household, within his own family, and He promised that the house of David would stand and it would be renewed throughout the ages.

26. The Lord our God promised to make the children of Israel like the grains of sand upon the shore, like the stars in the heavens.

27. He promised to redeem His children for the generations, to call them forth and make them stand before the nations of the world as His adopted children, as the children of the creator and the children of Heaven.

28. "When the kings of Israel rebelled against the Lord and began worshipping the Baals of the fields, when they started leading the children of Israel astray, still the Lord our God remained faithful.

29. He rebuked his children as a father would rebuke his son.

30. He chastened his children and corrected them so that they would remember the love that the Lord God had for his children, and the children returned to the Lord.

31. We turned back to the Lord, and we heard the words of the holy prophets.

32. We returned to His holy land, and we returned to the worship of the Lord our God.

33. We made the sacrifices upon the altar of the Lord even unto our own deaths and the death of our Lord, the Christ, the one who was called Jesus."

34. But at the mention of the Christ's name, the blind beggars cried out as one.

35. They wailed and gnashed their teeth.

36. They tore their clothes, and they fell upon the ground, dead.

37. A silence fell upon the land, a silence like no other.

38. The world itself refused to breathe.

39. The blind beggars lay still upon the ground, their corrupted scrolls and their corrupted copies lying upon their breasts.

40. Presently a shuffling came from behind me.

41. When I turned I saw the First Man, his leprous bindings blowing in a wind that did not blow upon the earth.

42. He knelt down beside the first blind beggar, pulled him into his arms, and lifted him high.

43. He spoke in the language of the angels, beseeching the Lord Most High, and the Lord answered his request and breathed life back into the blind beggar.

44. The First Man set him back upon the ground, and the man resumed his copying.

45. Once again he held the corrupted scroll in one hand while his other hand copied the lies onto another scroll.

46. As before, the First Man lifted a second blind beggar to the heavens, beseeching the Lord Most High for a miracle, and again the Lord answered, restoring life to one who would only corrupt the words of the Lord.

47. I ran to the First Man, and stood before him, blocking his path.

48. "Stop!" I cried out to him.

49. "In the name of our Lord God you must stop this abomination!"

50. The First Man only looked at me and said, "The words shall endure."

51. I shouted to him, "They are not the words of the Lord!"

52. Again, he said, "The words shall endure."

53. A third time, and with great anguish, I raised my arms to the Lord and cried out to the First Man, "The words upon those scrolls are corrupted!
54. They are not the words of our Lord God!"

55. And again the First Man said, "The words shall endure."

56. At this I was taken up into the heavens, brought high upon the hands of the Lord God to draw witness to the final events that would transpire.

18

The Revelation of Simon
Chapter 9

1. I was placed at the seat of honor within the Throne Room of the Lord God Almighty.

2. I was seated at the right hand of the throne of the Lord God Almighty, and I cast my eyes down, too afraid to look.

3. I looked to the floor of the Throne Room of the Lord, but the Lord God Almighty Himself came and lifted my face high.

4. He allowed me to witness the glory of His passing before me as the wind that drifts upon the face of the earth, and it was full of His unending glory.

5. The Heavenly beings arrayed throughout the Throne Room bowed at the Lord God Almighty's

passing before them.

6. They shrank from His sight, but He held my head high; He allowed me the peace of His glory, the stillness of his wonder, the love of His being as He did not allow it to the Heavenly hosts arrayed throughout the room.

7. Upon returning to the throne, the Lord God Almighty raised His arms, and the Heavenly host were seated all about Him.

8. He then breathed upon the banquet table, and the Earth came to life upon it.

9. The waters of the Jordan, the hills of olives, and the roads of the Romans all filled the table.

10. We watched as the people upon the Earth went about their lives, birthing and dying, marrying and being given in marriage, loving and fighting, honoring the Lord God Almighty and cursing His Holy Name.

11. And as we watched the people of the Earth daily living their lives, I saw a shadow cross upon the water.

12. It was the shadow of a man, a shadow I had seen many times upon this journey, the shadow of

a man who witnessed the good yet spoke only evil.

13. The shadow of the Witness passed from the water and crossed upon the ground.

14. It passed through the valleys and the hills.

15. It passed over the cities and the fields.

16. It passed across the people of the Lord God Almighty, and it passed across the Jews and the Gentiles alike.

17. Wherever it passed, I saw the people's hearts become heavy, burdened with the knowledge of the gods and the cruelty of the world around them.

18. As the shadow passed across the surface of the earth, the hearts of every firstborn from every family everywhere, both Jew and Gentile, those following the Way and those who rejected His sacrifice, they all died within their bodies.

19. They were left as empty shells upon the earth, living and working, loving and dying, but never again truly alive.

20. Then the First Man stepped upon the earth, and he traveled slowly through the darkness, walking from town to town, and touching the souls of everyone he passed.

21. His rags dragged behind him, and the pesti-

lence of his youth engulfed his body as flies upon a corpse.

22. Everywhere he traveled, the people stepped away as if repulsed by his very presence.

23. But a few, a very small few, those whose hearts truly burned for the Lord before the dark presence slew their souls, those few approached the First Man and were healed.

24. Their souls were lit again, and they burned with the light of a thousand stars upon the midnight earth.

25. They gained many disciples who heard the word of the Lord and grew in their faith, grew in their love for each other and for the Lord our God.

26. The Lord God Almighty in Heaven suddenly clapped His hands, and a sound like the thunder of a midnight storm echoed across the earth.

27. And it was good.

19

The Revelation of Simon
Chapter 10

1. Though doing the good work, those souls that had been reborn for the Lord became like a shining beacon to the Evil One.

2. When the darkness had finally passed from across the face of the earth, brushed aside by the thunder clap of the Lord God Almighty, a second pestilence arose.

3. A cloud swirled at the four edges of the earth, a cloud the likes of which had not been seen since the dawning of the new age.

4. Within that cloud were the bodies of countless fleas.

5. They swarmed like an army, massing their bod-

ies upon the four corners of the earth as they prepared to strike at the Lord's people.

(DAMAGED TEXT – VERY SMALL SECTION)

7. his broken and bandaged body like a reed before the oncoming storm.

8. He stood there and proclaimed the Word of the Lord God Almighty, and the fleas roared their anger.

9. Suddenly one of the Hosts of Heaven proclaimed, "It has begun!", and the fleas were released.

10. They attacked every nation on earth and afflicted the people of every tribe.

11. They swarmed across the people's bodies, attacked their genitals, grew across their arms and legs, and took up residences within the hair atop

(DAMAGED TEXT – VERY SMALL SECTION)

12. if such a thing were even possible, and this revelation of the Lord our God has shown it to be true.

13. Everywhere the fleas infested the land and the people hearts grew hard to the Lord our God.

14. The fleas turned the people from the Lord God Almighty and from His very Word.

15. They turned the land against the people, making the crops to fail and the animals to become sick and deathly.

16. The fleas swarmed across all waters, across the streams and the lakes, across the very seas themselves until not one body of water stood pure in the sight of the righteous.

17. There was not one place upon the earth from which to take a drink that had not been polluted.

18. The fleas infested the wine skins and the storehouses of grain.

19. They infested the hovels of the poor and the mansions of the wealthy.

(DAMAGED TEXT – VERY SMALL SECTION)

21. enduring the same calamity as those around him.

22. Suffering the same injustices as those who came before.

23. He stood strong in the face of such pain and

weeping, though, and he resisted the onslaught of the Evil One.

24. He spoke truth into the face of such destruction, and he held firm in his faith in the Lord our God.

25. In that, however, he was all but alone, for the peoples of the earth fled from the Lord God Almighty.

26. They blasphemed His Holy Name, casting blame upon Him for the destruction that had been wrought by the Evil One.

27. Almost to a man, they cast aside the words of the Law and the Prophets.

28. They cast aside the prayers of the righteous.

29. They cast aside their love for one another and for their God, and they turned toward the lusts of the world.

30. They turned toward the lies of the unrighteous that say there is no God, that trust in the ways of men and not the ways of God, that blaspheme His Holy Name.

31. The First Man walked through the storm of fleas, his arms raised high in praise to the Lord our God.

32. He prayed for the Lord's blessings.

33. He prayed for the Lord's righteousness.

34. He prayed for the Lord God Almighty's healing upon the land.

35. The Lord God in Heaven, the Mighty One seated upon the throne of righteousness, raised His hands into the air and clapped with a mighty thunder that shook the throne room and shook the banquet table and shook the very ground upon which the First Man walked.

36. And the fleas fell dead upon the earth.

37. And it was good.

The Revelation of Simon
Chapter 11

1. Then all was still for an age, and for a second age.

2. The people lived their lives upon the earth, loving and being loved, marrying and being given in marriage, and few gave heed to the First Man standing at the center of the earth and praising the Lord our God for the good that He wrought upon the people, upon His people and upon those who had rejected His Holy Word.

3. And the First Man wept.

4. He wept not at their rebellion but also at the distance that had grown up within their hearts, at the absolute disregard with which the people held His

Holy Word.

5. They knew Him not.

6. And as the First Man's tears fell upon the earth, the Witness grew up again as seeds upon the ground.

7. He grew up at the First Man's feet, in the shadow of the First Man's praises to the Lord our God, but he refused to heed them.

8. He heard the First Man uttering praises to the Lord our God, but he rejected the Light of the First Man's testimony to the peoples, and he went out again unto the earth.

9. He whispered to the peoples of the earth, and at first I could not hear what was said.

10. He whispered to still more people, he drifted through the cities and the nations, speaking words of his own understanding to the people he met, to all the people he encountered.

11. He whispered words that blasphemed the Lord God Almighty, and when I turned to His Holy throne in Heaven, I saw the tears that were shed for every lost child upon the earth.

12. As the Witness wandered the earth, whisper-

ing to all the people, the blasphemy of the peoples of the earth became like a chorus from the ground, a chorus that was lifted up to Heaven, if even such a thing were possible, and this revelation of the Lord God Almighty has shown it to be true.

13. They lifted their blasphemy to the Heavens, and I heard it clearly upon the wind, that the Lord God Almighty was returning again, that He was coming with the midnight sun, that He was returning as the Morning Star.

14. My heart leaped for joy, for surely this was a testimony of the Lord God Almighty, a revelation given to the righteous themselves.

15. It was surely proof that the Witness had finally turned his wicked heart to the Lord.

16. But still the Lord our God wept upon the throne.

17. The tears fell like rain upon the banquet table, and the earth began to tremble at His sorrow.

18. As the Witness went from one nation to another, the floodgates of the heavens were opened.

19. People's hearts began to look to the sky, but the skies only let loose the sorrow-filled rain storms of the Lord our God.

20. The people's hearts began to shine with the light of righteousness, but their light was returned to them as darkness upon the earth.

21. The people prayed to the Lord our God, but He would not hear them.

22. Their prayers went unanswered.

23. Suddenly, the Witness turned his face to the sky, and as if they were of one mind and one body, the peoples of the earth turned their faces to the sky also.

24. In silence they stood, watching the sky.

25. They prayed to the sky to see the face of the Lord's return.

26. His words were upon their lips.

27. His face was upon their hearts.

28. The Witness shouted to the heavens, "Behold, the Lord!"

29. But the Lord did not come.

30. The Witness shouted a second time to the heavens, "Behold, the Lord!"

31. But again, the Lord did not come.

32. The Witness shouted a third time to the heavens, "Behold, the Lord!"

33. And the morning dawned with the rooster's crow.

34. But this time, when the Lord did not come, the people's faces turned from the sky.

35. They cast their gaze upon the ground, and they turned their backs on the Lord our God.

36. At that moment, the Heavenly creatures stood still, and there was unending silence throughout the heavens.

37. The Lord God Almighty sat upon His throne, weeping for the death laid out upon the banquet table before Him.

38. His tears flowed throughout the heavens, running across the banquet table, around the mountains of the earth, and across the dead walking upon the face of the earth.

39. And it was not good.

21

The Revelation of Simon
Chapter 12

1. The people of the Earth went about their lives, being born and dying, marrying and being given in marriage, but they no longer turned their hearts to the Lord our God.

2. Corruption grew up within their hearts, and they began to change black as night.

3. Their sin and wickedness poisoned their bodies.

4. Its roots spread into their arms and legs; it sprouted within their souls.

5. The wickedness drained like blood from their eyes, but they did not see.

6. They did not see the sin of themselves, nor did they see the sins of their neighbors.

7. They were blinded by the corruption pouring from within.

8. The Lord our God spread His arms wide above the banquet table.

9. He beckoned the people to return to Him, but they refused to see.

10. They were blinded by the rivers of blood pouring from their eyes, from the corruption that had so stolen their hearts, that they would not even acknowledge that the Lord our God was there, that he was calling them to Him, that He was beckoning them to return to their first love.

11. The Lord wept.

12. And the peoples upon the Earth took up their swords.

13. They raised their plowshares as weapons upon the winds.

14. Those that had no tools or weapons at hand took up stones from the ground.

15. The peoples of the Earth turned as one and set upon the First Man.

16. They struck him with all their might, tearing

his limbs, wrenching apart his body, tearing apart his leprosy-infested bindings.

17. They took the twelve pieces of his rotting flesh and they flung them across all the tribes of Israel. They scattered his blood and they scattered his flesh upon the ground, and then they trampled upon them until all corners of the world were stained red.

18. The Lord God Almighty turned His back upon the Earth, and it was not good.

22

The Revelation of Simon Chapter 13

1. All was silent in Heaven.

2. The Lord God Almighty left His throne and walked past the banquet table spread out before the heavenly creatures, and as he did a darkness fell upon the Earth.

3. Everywhere His shadow fell, the creatures of the Earth died.

4. The birds flew but did not live.

5. The flowers bloomed but did not live.

6. The fish swam but did not live.

7. And the people walked upon the face of the blackened Earth but did not live.

8. After the Lord our God left the throne room

and the banquet table, and after the peoples of the Earth had trampled upon the First Man and spread his body and blood to the four corners, and after the Heavenly hosts turned their backs upon the scenes spread before us, only then did the Witness begin once again to walk upon the Earth.

9. His steps were like water upon the rivers of blood, washing away the last stains of the First Man's blood upon the ground, and everywhere he went the people no longer spoke the name of the Lord God Almighty.

10. They cast aside His Holy Word and took up a new word.

11. Where once there was light, now there was darkness, but the Witness told them the new darkness was good.

12. Where once there was the wisdom of the righteous, now there was only the wisdom of fools, and the Witness told them the new wisdom was good.

13. Where once there was the love of the Lord our God, now there was only the love of their fellow

men, and the Witness told them the new love was good.

14. The directions became confused, and the path of the righteous became many, and the peoples of the world turned as one away from the Lord our God.

15. The Witness led them to the edge of the world, and the peoples followed.

16. He ushered them into a new world, a world no longer flowing with milk and honey, a world ruled by men with no room in their hearts for God.

17. The banquet table emptied as the last follower of The Way stepped off its edge to go into eternal darkness.

18. I stood in the empty throne room, weeping before the deserted table of the Lord, and I cried out to the Lord my God, but there was no answer.

19. I was left alone for an eternity, weeping for the silence that endured in Heaven.

20. After a time and a second time, I looked up again and found myself standing in the Taberna-

cle, His Holy Dwelling Place in the desert.

21. The four doors were opened to the desert beyond, to the night on which I had departed to seek the face of the Lord.

22. The words of His mouth were upon my tongue, and my witness was ready to go forth unto the peoples of the world.

23. I had been set aside for the Lord God Almighty's purpose, and I knew that I must go forth and spread the word that I had received, this Revelation of the end of days, this testimony of the things that are to come but must never be allowed to transpire.

24. I saw the peoples of this world forsaking the Lord our God and stepping into an eternity of their own desolation.

25. May it never come to pass.

3

Commentary & Analysis

23

Commentary & Analysis
Prologue

To begin my commentary, I will write briefly about the entire Revelation. This Revelation of Simon is almost as long as the Revelation of John that we currently have in the Protestant Bible. John's Revelation is approximately 10,000 words, and this revelation of Simon is approximately 8,500 words. However there is no way to know for certain how long Simon's revelation was in its original form because of the damaged pieces of text it now contains. However, an educated guess can be offered that what we have remaining is approximately what Simon wrote originally, because even though portions of this text are damaged, the damaged portions are actually quite small when compared to the entirety of this full Revelation.

Regarding the authorship, there is no way to know which Simon is being referred by the text. The annotation that this is Simon the son of Cuphythis is not helpful when the father's name is so foreign to what we know from historical documents. Simon's was a common enough name in the first and second centuries, but the father's name is quite unusual. It seems to have most in common with Greek names of the period, but the Revelation itself has more of a Hebrew tenor to it than a Greek one, especially noted by the Hebrew text itself. For example the author of this Revelation displays, especially in the earliest chapters, an anger and familiarity with the destruction of the temple in Jerusalem and with the Jewish revolts of the late first century. A Greek author would likely be far less interested in or bothered by those events, or at the very least he would portray a different attitude regarding them.

In overall layout, this revelation of Simon is also similar to the Revelation of John. It begins with Simon retreating off by himself and receiving the Revelation just as John did. From there the first portion of the Revelation has Simon interacting with various heavenly beings inside of a desert tabernacle. When that first part concludes, he begins a journey through portions of history and through various visions that he is receiving from God. In stark contrast to the Revelation of John, however, the Revelation of Simon does not end with Jesus's glorious return to Earth. But it ends on a much more horrific scene of the Lord turning his back on all the people of Earth as they retreat into the darkness. That ending seems to suggest a much different intent for the writing of this Revelation. Where John was seeking to encourage and to uplift the early Christians, this revelation of Simon seems more of a warning, especially to those Christians who might be seeking to uphold the Jewish traditions or distort the newer traditions being established by the Christians.

So that you can better understand how I write this commentary, let me explain the way these texts were compiled. Each of the texts is made up of several scrolls bound together. This Revelation of Simon was one of the easiest to translate and compile because the scrolls had not come loose from each other. Some of the other texts within this group will take me much longer to organize and translate because the bindings have come loose and I am unsure which ones must remain together. For people who will be reading this commentary it will not feel like biblical writings that we are used to reading in the 21st century. Our modern biblical texts were compiled between the 4th and 8th centuries the way that we have them today, especially regarding the chapters and verses with which they have been divided. This text we have before us and the others that are part of this same collection come from a period in time prior to those chapter-and-verse delineations. The chapter-and-verse delineations now contained within this text are of my own devising based on an overall understanding of the thematic material contained within. Understand that there were no chapter divisions in the original text. I have placed chapter divisions where they seem most natural based on the context of the scrolls, and no one should read more into those divisions than what I intend, and that is merely an easier reading and discussion of the text they contain.

Though I have had to remain in hiding for my own safety to complete this work, I am quite grateful for the scholarly assistance I have received from several brave souls in America and around the world. There is no doubt that this text originates from the 1st and 2nd centuries because one brave soul, against her better judgment, was able to take a portion of the scrolls that I forwarded and analyze it with some of the latest scientific techniques on my behalf. I am eternally grateful for her bravery in that regard. That was the greatest confirmation I could have had that I am dealing with some of the most significant historical texts that have been unearthed in the last 75 years. Though this is only the first of the texts that I have been able to translate and compile I will continue in the best of my ability in my work to make the rest of the documents in this treasure available to the public. This scholarship is too important and must be known, no matter the danger to my own person.

24

―――――

Commentary & Analysis
Chapter 1

I begin my commentary with the first chapter of the Revelation of Simon. The structure of this first chapter should be quite familiar to anyone who knows the Revelation of John. Simon begins this chapter with a downcast heart after witnessing a terrible tragedy. He retreats to the desert where he fasted for 39 days, at the end of which he receives a vision from the Lord. Though he is initially frightened and his description of the Lord is quite detailed, the Lord reassures Simon, and Simon considers that reassurance the first sign the Lord gave him.

The first paragraph begins with Simon expressing a curse upon anyone who would alter the meaning of these words or of this entire revelation. The curious thing about this curse is that he is casting down upon the one who would alter these words the same curse that is granted to the Witness of the Lord. But at this point in the revelation, no one reading it would understand the character of the Witness of the Lord. It is not until completing a reading of this revelation that someone would see the curse the Witness of the Lord receives is to be cast out of the Lord's sight into eternal darkness with the other apostates. Simon also grants to the faithful servant a blessing of the fullness of the measure that is to come. This is a fairly standard introduction to a piece of revelatory text from the early Christian movement and merely confirms that this writing is in accord with other writings of the same period.

The second paragraph is so much shorter than either the 1st or 3rd that are around it. Its message is very simple, that someone should remain strong in his faith for the time is near. What is not stated in that paragraph is whose or what's time is actually near. This is because whatever message Simon was conveying to the Christians of his time would have been known by those same Christians. Based upon other texts of the time, it can most likely be said that the time to which Simon refers is the return of Jesus to Jerusalem, an event the early Christians expected would happen at any moment.

Paragraph 3 begins to tell the story of Simon's path through this revelation. What is immediately fascinating with this paragraph is Simon's use of the term "the Way" to refer to himself and his fellow believers. The use of this term would place the writing of this revelation at a fairly early point in the spread of the gospel of Jesus when the disciples were simply known as "the Way." The rest of the paragraph seems to be a condemnation of the Jews of his time. There is much to be said in this paragraph about the Lord letting loose his wrath on a stubborn and wicked generation, echoing the same type of terminology that we find in the four Gospels that Jesus would have used to refer to the Jews of his time. That is further reinforced by Simon specifying that these people were the ones who committed adultery with the golden calf, a reference to Exodus 32. This is a blatant reference to the Israelites following the Exodus when Moses was communing with God on Mount Sinai. There the Israelites donated their gold so that an idol could be fashioned from it for them to worship while Moses was away. The next sentence is equally damning to the Jews of Simon's time when he says that the people could not see the serpent and be cleansed from their wickedness and unrighteousness. Again this is a reference to a story that took place during the Exodus, this time from Numbers 21. The Israelite camp was invaded by poisonous snakes, and a totem with a snake wrapped around it was placed in their midst. All the Israelites had to do to be healed of their sickness was to turn and look at that totem with the snake on it. We are familiar with this same totem today because it is used in medical practice in the United States and around the world to represent professions of healing. For Simon to say that the people of his time were blinded and could not see that totem so they could be healed is as much to say that their own stubborn hearts kept them from turning to the Lord. That statement is immediately followed by another statement that those rebellious people were swallowed up by the earth. Again this is a reference to an exodus story in which the rebellious people who were following Moses were swallowed up by the earth, as described in Numbers 16. Simon concludes this paragraph by stating that it was a crushing vindication for the Lord to wipe away the memories of these people and their hard hearts because they were disloyal to him. What's interesting about that is that he actually seems to be referencing different points in history during the first century. It can be guessed from the beginning of this paragraph and the desolation that Simon witnessed on Mount Sinai that he is referring to the destruction of the Jewish temple in the latter half of the first century, but the end of this paragraph seems to imply that the people are receiving their punishments because they showed disloyalty to "him" when "he" was with them. That can best be seen as a reference to Jesus's time on earth, the priests rejecting Jesus, and the eventual crucifixion of Jesus.

Simon next goes out into the desert to fast and pray. This is a clear allusion to Jesus going into the desert to fast and pray and be tempted by Satan. Simon writes that he cries out to the Lord for these 39 days and finally on the 40th day the Lord hears his cry and asks who is seeking Him. Again in verse 11 we have a reference to Simon as the son of Cuphythis. This gives us no more context as to who Simon is or who his father might be or if the name is simply a pseudonym for some other follower of the Way, perhaps a mentor. Verse 13 has God replying to Simon with the ubiquitous "I am" statement. After making that statement the earth becomes as silent as it was during the hour before creation, another allusion to the Old Testament Genesis and Exodus books, which is a common point of reference throughout much of Simon's revelation. Simon immediately expresses unworthiness to God, and the Lord replies with the odd sentiment "I have sent whom I have sent."

The first chapter I have chosen to end with verse 17 and Simon's pronouncements that he has received the first sign. Several of the early chapters in this revelation end with a declaration of a sign. This is not unusual for revelatory writings in the first and second centuries.

△△△

Verse 1:

- Cuphythis: An unknown name, not seen anywhere else in ancient text. The form is more closely Greek than Hebrew.
- Jesus, the Nazarene: The only reference to

"the Nazarene" throughout this text. It appears to be a clarifying statement at the beginning of the book to ensure there will be no confusion before the Revelation continues.

- God Almighty (here and throughout): literally, "great god"

Verse 3:

- Millstones: literally "crushing stones"; translated as "millstones"
- Purgatory: literally "Sheol," where all the dead go before God's judgment

Verse 5:

- "the Way": 1st-century reference to followers of Christ; modern form is "Christian"; also in chapters 9 and 13

Verse 6:

- "Golden Calf": Exodus 32

Verse 7:

- "the serpent to cleanse": Numbers 21

Verse 8:

- "swallowed whole by the Earth": Numbers 16
- "Lord our God" (here and throughout): literally "Shema Yisrael"

Verse 9:

- "wiped away": literally "crushed into nothingness"

Verse 13:

- "I am" (here and throughout): literally "Ehyeh asher ehyeh," or "I am that I am"

25

Commentary & Analysis
Chapter 2

The second chapter tells the story of Simon's encounter in the desert wilderness with the four sons of God. He finds in the desert the tabernacle of the Lord, a clear reference to the Old Testament tabernacle that went with the Israelites as they travelled throughout the desert and then was placed beside David's camp until Solomon built the final temple in Jerusalem. The beings referenced in this chapter as appearing like sons of God are most likely angels. Their placement at the four doorways of the tabernacle further reinforces their duties as guards within God's holy house, stationed at the four corners of the world. This chapter is the first of several that relate various visions Simon receives from within the temple of the Lord. Each vision is led by a different angel who shows Simon different points in history.

Verse 1 begins with Simon standing in the stillness of the night from the previous chapter and hearing someone cry out to the Lord. That person who is crying out is never identified directly, but the most logical person to express that cry would be Simon himself. That interpretation is reinforced by the fact that he is alone, that he was expressing extreme sadness in the previous chapter, and that he had been crying out to the Lord before the Lord found him. Interestingly Simon does not have to go anywhere to reach the temple; it simply appears around him along with the four angels. Those four guardian angels are dressed as warriors of the first century, most likely images that Simon would have seen as he was watching the temple be destroyed by the Romans. The only piece of their description that does not seem to correlate with a Roman soldier analogy would be the blue sashes across the Angels' gold breastplates. A blue sash like that in the first century would have indicated someone of royalty, which fits quite well with the rest of the description of the Angels themselves.

As Simon goes on to describe those angels it is interesting to note the different placements of each one's sword. One angel has buried his sword in the ground, the second angel is pointing his sword at Simon's chest, and the third one has his sword raised above his head as he expresses praise to God. The placement of those swords is a clear allusion to the stories the three angels each relate to Simon. The angel pointing its sword at Simon's chest will be showing him the world as it exists at that point in time. The angel with its sword buried in the ground will be telling Simon a story from the past, and the angel with its sword held high will be telling Simon a story from the future.

Verse 8 is especially interesting in that the Angel to the South entrance is standing with his sword held loose at his side and watching the other three angels, but his eyes are moving from west to east, which is opposite that of nature. His revelation is revealed to Simon in chapter 5, and it is his revelation that is the most different from the other three. It is his Revelation that takes Simon on the journey away from the Tabernacle. That Journey seems to be one of introspection and discovery for Simon, and the angel viewing the

Tabernacle opposite that of nature is likely fore-shadowing that internal journey that Simon will undergo in chapter five. That difference also high-lights the Angel to the South as that is the one who first begins speaking and asking who is calling out to the Lord. Interestingly enough, each time the angel asks that question it is the other Angels in-side the Tabernacle that answer when the text ear-lier clearly suggests it was Simon who was the one calling out to the Lord as he wandered the desert. The response that the Angel to the North gives when he says "It is I" is reminiscent of many of the Old Testament descriptions of God stating of him-self "I am" or "I am that I am."

After the Angel to the North reveals himself as the one who is crying out to the Lord, he presses the point of his sword against Simon's chest and Simon feels the burning in his chest as the word of the Lord pierces his soul. That phrase "the word of the Lord" could have either one of two interpre-tations. It could be referencing the Old Testament scrolls of the Laws and the Prophets as the word that was given to Moses and the Israelites, or it could be interpreted as the Book of John interprets it as being the Word that was with God from the beginning, in other words Jesus Christ. The context of the chapter and the context of the verse do not seem to give a clear indication which interpretation of that phrase Simon means. For the sake of consistency within my translation, and because so much of what Simon writes contains so many allusions to the Old Testament, I have chosen to interpret the phrase with reference to the Law and the Prophets instead of to the text of the Gospel of John.

Simon follows the Angel of the North out of the Tabernacle and begins a journey through the Jordan River Valley. This journey to the Jordan River Valley echoes another Old Testament story, this one from the book of Ezekiel. Instead of being a river filled with water and life, however, the Jordan has become a dry riverbed that is baking in the heat of the sun. Not only that but it is filled with the bones of what are most likely the people of Israel. This vivid and horrifying description is clearly an allusion to the destruction of the temple in Jerusalem and the dried wasteland it was left following that event. Much of this revelation of Simon has a harsh critique of the Jews of his time and the experiences that they had before, during, and following the destruction of the Temple. That is further reinforced by verse 16 pointing out that among the bones of the witnesses in the dry riverbed are the shards of 12 lampstands, a clear allusion to the 12 tribes of Israel.

As Simon walks through this riverbed following the Angel of the North, the Earth is shaken 3 times. Each time that happens the bones and the shards of the lampstand leap into the air, most likely as an effect of the wind pounding the ground so strongly. The "million tongues of flames" referenced in verse 20 are an allusion to the tongues of the Holy Spirit that were given to the 12 disciples following Jesus' ascension into Heaven. This story seems to be clearly indicating that if the people of Israel who were struck down following the destruction of the Temple would only allow themselves to be filled with the Holy Spirit that they could come together as one people and become even stronger and mightier than they had been in the past when they were nothing but bones scattered across the Jordan River Valley. Again, a harsh critique of 1st-century Jews.

Following the resurrection of the people of Israel by the power of the infilling of the Holy Spirit,

Simon sees the Angel to the North pointing to the end of the Jordan River Valley where the First Man is standing and watching. This First Man character is an interesting literary device throughout this revelation as he accompanies Simon through much of the journey, but most of the time from a distinctive distance from him. This first appearance of the First Man is also quite alarming if the reader does not know where the entire story goes. He is clearly presented as a sick and frail person who must be avoided. The reference to him as the First Man and the later description of him walking through the Garden of Eden would seem to imply that he is an Adam figure, possibly even supposed to be Adam himself following the fall from the Garden of Eden. He is clearly a witness to everything going on throughout Simon's revelation though he does not share the same characteristics as the character of the Witness that appears throughout the revelation and who writes down what he sees and shares that with the people of the world, though a corrupted version of the revelation. This character of the First Man presented here gives the appearance of one who cannot be trusted even though by the conclusion of the Revelation the First Man is the one most trusted by Simon. It is the later Witness who proves to be the more untrustworthy of the two. That literary transposition appears several times throughout Simon's revelation, of having one thing that the reader expects to happen be turned on its head so that it was the wrong interpretation when first encountered; the correct interpretation throughout much of the revelation is the one that comes later, when the first interpretation is flipped around 180 degrees. That is especially reinforced as the First Man walks away spreading pestilence wherever he goes, but in later chapters the First Man is the character bringing life to the people whom the Witness has led astray. Again this chapter ends with a statement that the second sign was received.

△△△

Verse 1:

- "desolate stillness": literally "realm of silent death"

Verse 3:

- "Tabernacle" (here and throughout): literally "mishkan," meaning "residence" or "dwelling place" of the Lord

Verse 4:

- "Sons of God" (here and throughout): sons of "Elohiym," the same language used in Job to reference the angels (including Satan) who presented themselves before God

Verse 6:

- "Living God" (here and throughout): literally "Elohim Chayim"

Verse 8:

- "Almighty" (here and throughout): literally "Shadday"

Verse 9:

- "wilderness": literally "wild lands"

Verse 11:

- "Word of the Lord" (here and throughout): literally "memra," or the speech of God manifested through the physical world; it would mean that God came to life as living word; commonly used when God is speaking directly to a prophet

Verse 14:

- "fell away": dropped into the abyss

Verse 16:

- Twelve lampstands: the lampstands adorning the Temple of the Lord; see Exodus 25 and throughout John's Revelation

Verse 17:

- "mighty wind": strong, pounding wind
- "clapping with the joy of the righteous": literally "releasing holy thunder"

Verse 20:

- "Tongues of flame": as in Acts 2, literally "cloven tongues"; an allusion to a divine light, not meant to imply literal tongues

Verse 24:

- "Sovereign Lord": from "mamlakah," or "entire kingdom of the Lord"
- "life like you have never known before": can mean "changed life" or "opposite life" or "deeper life"; all imply a life completely different from any previous life

Verse 26:

- "cooked with the light of the new dawn's flame": meaning to be melted down in an oven, cooked past the point of death and into a completely new form; the imagery is most similar to a chrysalis but within the divine heat of a cooking oven

Verse 31:

- "First Man" (here and throughout): derivation of "Adam," which is more closely rendered "mankind"; "First Man" in this text is given the proper noun form and meant to imply a specific man without a name of his own who is living at a particular time in history; for purposes of this translation, I have rendered it as the proper noun form "First Man," as a character within this Revelation

Verse 33:

- "soul" (here and throughout): "nephesh" meaning "essence of the living person": rendered here as "soul"
- "Winter's death": the season of death (dormancy) that precedes life

26

Commentary & Analysis
Chapter 3

Chapter 3 is filled with some of the most vivid imagery of the entire revelation. That also makes this chapter one of the most challenging to translate based on the culture and times in which it was written and interpreting it to a modern audience. The setup of chapter 3 is very much the same as chapters 2 and 4. In fact the three chapters together can be viewed as a look at all of history. Chapter 2 is looking at the current state of affairs in the world during the time this Revelation was most likely written, immediately following the fall of the temple in Jerusalem. Chapter 3 is the past and a return to the Garden of Eden, or, as it is referred to in the chapter, Paradise. Chapter 4 contains vivid imagery of what can most likely be interpreted as the future on through to the end of time.

As with chapter 2, chapter 3 begins with Simon inside the Tabernacle of the Lord. This time however Simon has just been returned from his travels in chapter 2, and the sword of the word of the Lord is still within his chest. When the angel removes that sword from his chest he is left with a burning that could most likely be interpreted as a longing to have that word of the Lord put back inside of him. Again the angel to the South asks who was crying out into the wilderness, and Simon answers that it is he. The angel to the West removes his sword from the ground and places the point of it to Simon's head. There is imagery to be found here in the placement of the sword of the Angel of the lord inside each chapter. Chapter 2 has the sword being placed inside Simon's chest, which is the seat at which people today believe that their souls reside. In chapter 3 having the sword placed into Simon's head is a clear allusion to the mind of Simon being engaged for this spiritual journey, although today we interpret the heart as the resting place of a person's soul. Chapter 4 continues this allusion as Simon is never given the sword of the word of the Lord but instead reaches forward to grasp it from the angel. Interestingly, the text does not reveal that Simon actually gets the sword or even touches it, only that he reaches for it.

When Simon and the angel cross the threshold of the Tabernacle they are immediately transported to what Simon refers to as Paradise, but has clear imagery of what we refer to now as the Garden of Eden. We see in this paragraph the angels of the Lord guarding the entrance to the garden with their swords swinging back and forth to block people from entering. We see the River of Life flowing through the garden, and we see all of the animals, interestingly including the serpent, once again inside the garden. Simon clearly knows his Genesis history as well as his spiritual grounding because when the serpent passes by and beckons Simon to follow him, Simon instead stomps his heel upon the serpent's head. Instead of stopping the serpent, however, there is a second serpent that shows up, and then a third after the second is killed. Finally after striking the third serpent, Simon looks at the angel and sees the angel weeping for the dying serpent. Those tears for the death of the serpent are fascinating especially when looking at this character from Genesis from a modern perspective. Christians today generally view the serpent as an enemy and often refer to the serpent itself as the personification of Satan. This view of the serpent from this first century text, however, clearly shows a different interpretation of what that serpent was thought to be at the time. While it was not a creature to be trusted, the angel does not view it as a creature to be killed. Instead, its death warrants mourning.

Though Simon pleads for the angel to forgive him, there is nothing in the text that leads one to believe that the angel actually offers any forgiveness. Instead Simon flees into the garden beneath the feet of the angels of the Lord and follows the serpent who was beckoning him to follow in the first place. They pass all of the animals of the garden, and they pass the Tree of the Knowledge of Good and Evil. Interestingly, when they pass the Tree of Life, the fruit of everlasting life has become rotten on the vine, clearly implying that eternal life has not been harvested as it should have been. In an odd turn of events it is the serpent that weeps for the fruit of the Tree of Life as it is rotting on the vine.

When Simon and the serpent finally reach the mountain of the Lord they both bow down before the Lord, but it is the serpent that first begins two other praises to the Lord. Again this provides a different interpretation of who the serpent was thought to be in the first century, at least from within Simon's perspective.

As the chapter concludes, the First Man makes another appearance. Again he is wearing the wrappings of a leper, and Simon can smell the stench of death upon him. The First Man wraps his arms around Simon in what can probably best be described as a hug and then asks Simon to proclaim his witness to all the nations. That witness however is vague because we don't know if the witness to be proclaimed is the serpent praising God and bowing before the Throne or if it is the rotten fruit on the vine of the Tree of Life or if it is the witness of the condition of the First Man himself. The best interpretation for the way the chapter is written is that Simon is actually being asked to proclaim everything he has seen.

Once again this chapter ends with the declaration of another sign being given.

△△△

Verse 2:

- "Burned": a painful searing, as from a hot coal

Verse 7:

- "to my head": literally, "at the seat of my soul"; 1st-century Christians and Jews believed the soul to reside in a person's head whereas modern-day Christians usually gesture to the center of the body, to the "heart," when gesturing to the soul

Verse 10:

- "paradise": literally, "the place of the beginning" or "Eden"

Verse 11:

- "River of Life": literally, "waters from which life flowed" or "living waters"

Verse 25:

- "destruction of its branch": the description is both present, "the branch that is withering," and past, "the branch that withered," implying that the destruction began a long time ago and is still going on

Verse 28:

- "silken river": implying a voice so smooth and rapturous as to be beyond compare with anything other than a finely spun cloth of water; this exact wording is unique to Biblical writings as it is seen nowhere else in Scripture, not even throughout the rest of this Revelation

Verse 35:

- "utter death": the word implies both "death" and "destruction"

Verse 36:

- "empty": literally, "vacant" or "with no soul remaining"

27

Commentary & Analysis
Chapter 4

As chapter 2 is a revelation of the way things currently are at the time that Simon is writing this in the first century, and as chapter 3 is a revelation of the past, of the way things were and how people got to where they were, so chapter 4 is a revelation of the things to come, of the future and of the end of time. This chapter begins the same way and with much of the same writing as chapters 2 and 3. Simon is standing in the temple once again and crying out at what he has just seen. The angel to the South once again asks who cries out to the Lord, and it is another angel, this time the one to the East, that responds positively. Unlike the first two angels, however, this third angel does not actually touch its sword to Simon. Instead Simon moves forward and tries to grasp the angel's sword. There is nothing in the text to indicate whether Simon is successful in his attempts to grasp the angel's sword. This Revelation also begins differently than the previous two because there is no crossing of the threshold into the world beyond the Tabernacle. Following the angel's praise of the Lord, the angel and Simon are simply passed through the curtain and stand upon a frozen shore.

This frozen world in which Simon and the angel find themselves is unique in all of scripture. There is no place like this throughout any of the Old or New Testament. It is possible that in his travels Simon had come across a frozen shoreline much like this. If that is the case it seems to indicate that Simon was someone who traveled in the northern edges of the Roman Empire. Though an interesting bit of information to keep in mind regarding the author, it is not something that can be said with any certainty. I do, however, plan to keep this information in mind as I translate and research the other texts I uncovered. The possibility exists that more such details might emerge regarding the author himself.

This frozen shoreline however is not dead but teeming with life beneath the surface of the frozen water. Harkening back to the Exodus story of Moses leading the Israelites, Simon ventures into the frozen waters and sees them part before him. The angel's description of what is being seen quite literally lets the reader know that this is a revelation of the end of time. In an entire book of Revelation that ends on such a catastrophic note, this is a glimpse of what could come at the end of time as a positive message to the Christians of the 1st century. Even so the message is weighed down because there are so many who have fallen away from the Lord before the end of time.

As Simon steps into the frozen water and the waves part before him, those who have been condemned fall to the left and those who are receiving paradise and who praise the Lord fall to the right, an interesting reversal compared against Simon's travels along the road in chapter 5, when the babies given to the evil one lie in the ditch at Simon's right, but the babies given over to God lie in the ditch at Simon's left. It is clear from this description of those on the left that they know and are fully aware of the judgment that has been laid upon them. As Simon moves through the frozen waters for 40 days and 40 nights, which is yet another clear allusion to both Jesus fasting in the wilderness for 40 days as well as Moses and the Israelites traversing the wilderness for 40 years, those people on the left who have been condemned grow far more numerous, and the righteous upon the right are far fewer until at the end of time there are no more righteous left to be found. It is the weight of the grief of those who have been condemned that finally brings Simon to a halt in his own despair.

Interestingly, it is at this point in Simon's despair that he once again finds the character of the First Man who, as I said, is likely a representation of Adam. Unlike the previous two encounters with the First Man, however, this time he is no longer dressed as a leper. He has been glorified with robes of the righteous and rings on his fingers representing the 12 tribes of Israel. Again there is a blatant mention from the First Man that what we are seeing is a revelation of the things to come, both the blessings and the curses that will be cast upon the Earth. The First Man, however, clearly states that it is he who will cast those blessings and those curses upon the Earth before the end of all time. This is especially interesting because it seems to imply that Adam, the first man (or "First Man," as he is referred to in this text) is also Jesus, the one who is giving these blessings and curses upon mankind. If so that is an interesting theological discussion that bears far more thought and consideration then I can currently give it at this point in time.

As with the previous chapters this one once again ends by stating that a sign has been given.

△△△

Verse 7:

- "longing within my soul": burning passion

Verse 8:

- "Lord, my Lord, oh Lord": literally three forms of the same name; the first is descriptive, the second possessive, and the third supplicating

Verse 10:

- "stars of ice": "burning points of light" upon the "frozen shore"; rendered as "stars of light"
- "frozen ecstasy": frozen in "extreme passion"

Verse 20:

- "tears of the fallen": literally, tears "of those who went before"; however, the context implies that those who went before have actually fallen away from the Lord; hence, the translation "tears of the fallen"

Verse 24:

- "rang out" within my soul: literally, "harmonized as two souls became one"
- "end of time": literally, "the omega of existence"; in contrast to the subtle difference of verse 35

Verse 35:

- "end of all things": literally, "the omega of all creatures"; in contrast to the subtle difference of verse 24

Commentary & Analysis
Chapter 5

Chapter 5 is the first portion of this revelation that contains damage to the text. As I stated previously, these scrolls were mostly well preserved over the course of time, but they are far from perfect. This portion of the scroll was severely damaged in several points. To reiterate how I am translating this text and dealing with the damaged portions of the scrolls, when there is a significantly large portion of scroll that has been damaged I am simply jumping ahead in the numbering of the verses by 10. When there is a smaller portion of text that has been damaged I am jumping ahead by 5 verses, and when there is a very small portion of text, likely a few words within a sentence, I am jumping ahead by only two verses.

Having said that, this chapter is especially unique compared to the four preceding chapters because this one begins a tale so unlike anything else that we have seen in the Revelation of John or even previously in this revelation of Simon's. This chapter contains a journey on which Simon embarks. It is a journey he does not wish to take until he receives the holy, red clothes the angels of the Lord leave for him within the Tabernacle. Or perhaps it was the Lord himself who left those clothes? Either way it is clearly shown that he cannot continue on this vision quest unless he is properly clothed. The use of the color red in itself is interesting because throughout the Bible that color is used as both a symbol of purity and a symbol of sin. Consider Isaiah 1:18 as well as Joshua 2:18 or Exodus 12:7. This particular story seems to give a similar dual interpretation of the color red. Simon is not allowed to continue on his journey until he is clothed in the red garments left for him in the Tabernacle, but he is also unworthy of continuing on his journey until later in the chapter he casts the same red garments over the cliff and is welcomed in the Embrace of the Lord. That seems to lead to the question of whether the clothes really were holy when they were given to Simon, whether Simon himself tainted the clothes by wearing them, or whether the clothes were always meant to be a sacrifice that allowed Simon to continue on his journey.

This chapter also contains some extremely disturbing imagery as Simon is walking on the pathway and is surrounded by the cries of children and infants. Some of those cries are in agony and some of those cries are in joy. It is most unfortunate that this portion of the text was so heavily damaged because the language seems to imply that neither the righteous children nor the condemned children greeted Simon positively.

The inclusion of the witch of Endor is also unique in this chapter. Again it is most unfortunate that so much of this chapter has been damaged when Simon first encounters the witch of Endor at her campfire. We have no way of knowing if she spoke with him, if she blessed (or cursed) him, or if she was even at the campfire at all. Later in the chapter, after he has cast aside the red garments and stands naked at the cliff, he seems quite afraid of her, and I believe we are missing much context because we are missing the interaction between the two of them when they first meet at the campfire.

The chapter begins in verse 1 with what seems to be a pause in the action of the revelation. Simon once again finds himself in the Tabernacle surrounded by the three angels who are like the son of God. The angel to the South, however, is no longer there, and the curtain behind him has been torn aside revealing an empty space that makes Simon quite afraid. He does not know what to do with the clothes that are lying upon the ground until the disembodied voice speaks from the other side of the Tabernacle and tells him to put on the clothes because he will walk upon Holy Ground. The voice is not identified, and it could be the angel or the Lord Himself. Even after putting on the holy garments, he is still afraid to enter the darkness. Once he finally does, he steps into a blinding snowstorm.

The snowstorm, much like the frozen shore, is also unique to this revelation. While we know that region of the Middle East could sometimes receive snow, no matter how unusual it might have been to the region it is quite unusual to see any reference to it in a piece of biblical texts. Again, either Simon's direct experience in life included some experience with snow or a snow storm or this truly was a revelatory experience given by God about something that Simon had never before experienced in his own life. The text through this portion is quite descriptive but does not lend credence to either explanation particularly one way or another.

In verse 11, Simon mentions that the path on which he is walking rests between the Holy Mountain and the desolate city. That reference to the desolate city was most likely a reference to the destroyed Jerusalem and the destroyed Temple. Interestingly, it is not until verse 23 that Simon reveals he did not know upon which path he was walking. He says that the Lord finally revealed it to him and that it was a well-worn path between the mountains of the Earth and the Temple of the Lord. The description of the path as being straight harkens back to Jesus's description of the road to Heaven being straight and narrow. The cries of the children that Simon hears upon this road are unique, however. The first children that he goes to see are those who have given themselves over to the Prince of Darkness. This seems to bring about a unique piece of theology implying that a child, particularly an infant child, could give himself or herself over to the Prince of Darkness willingly. That would seem to suggest, contrary to what some modern Christian theologians and denominations profess, that children do not receive any kind of probationary period but they actively seek out the Lord or seek out the Prince of Darkness at the time of their own choosing. That is a piece of theological discussion best saved for another time and a more appropriate space.

The children however are singing a song of mourning for the parents who abandoned them upon this road. Whether those parents actively abandoned them or the children were simply left behind is not revealed by the text. Simon shows his mercy and compassion upon these children as he stretches out his hand to lift them out of their misery. Unfortunately, as I said earlier, there is a significant portion of the text of this chapter that is missing, and we do not know what happened when he attempted to lift the children out of their misery. Assuming a parallel between this section and verses 39-43, however, it could be assumed that his attempt was unsuccessful.

Those same verses 39-43 discuss another group of children who are also singing a song of mourning, but interestingly enough, these children bear the mark of the sacrifice of the Passover Lamb upon their necks. That would seem to imply that these children were known by God but were still left abandoned along the side of the road. Again the theological implications of that are best left for another time when we can go into more depth upon such a weighty subject, but it would seem to imply a perception of childhood in the 1st century that is rather far removed from our modern perceptions of childhood spirituality.

It is at verse 49 that Simon comes upon the camp that is revealed to be the camp of the witch of Endor. Though we are only missing a small portion of text, there seems to be quite a bit that happened in these few missing verses between the time that he realizes the witch is watching him to the time that he references a person who does not hear his cry. One can only assume that the "he" referenced here is the Lord, but the text is uncertain as to why Simon's cries went unanswered.

When Simon reaches the end of the path he seems to have reached also the end of the world. He looks out into the darkness, or, as it could be interpreted, he looks out into the void. He knows that he must make himself naked and cast the holy red garments into the darkness, but he does not want to do that because he believes it to be blasphemy, even though he knows that's what the Lord wants of him. Interestingly, when he casts off those garments and tosses them into the abyss, he mentions that they have become tattered, even though nothing in the preceding text would indicate that he had done anything to make them tattered. Perhaps something happened to them in the portions of text we are missing?

The next few verses seem to imply that Simon was given a choice. Once he cast off his holy red garments he turns around and sees the witch of Endor at her campfire beckoning him to her. This makes him quite afraid, and when he turns away from her he is greeted by the Lord at the entrance to the Temple. The Lord embraces him and tells him that he is worthy, presumably because he did not follow the beckoning of the witch of Endor. This would seem to imply that the reader of this

Revelation is being given a very similar choice whether to continue on into the path of the Lord or to continue back to the witch of Endor who is waiting with a warm fire and a hot meal. Again the theological implications are quite profound and should be dealt with in much greater detail at another time.

∆∆∆

Verse 3:

- "red": associated in ancient times as both a symbol of sin as well as redemption; the stain of sin and the blood of the sacrifice; interestingly, Jewish clothing of the 1st century that was colored red was more often associated with women than with men because of the blood of the menstrual cycle

Verse 6:

- "darkness": "the black void"

Verse 8:

- "mountains of the Lord": alternatively, "holy mountains"; it is the plural form and meant in the generic sense, not the singular "mountain of the Lord" or "Holy Mountain," which is most often translated as Mt. Sinai in the Bible; contrast with verse 11

Verse 10:

- "fury": anger

Verse 11:

- "Holy Mountain": "mountain of the Lord"; alternatively, "Mt. Sinai"; however, for this translation, I stayed more literal to the meaning of the words themselves instead of allegorical

Verse 24:

- "well worn": literally, "trod down solid"

- "eternal torment": alternatively, "infinite pain"

Verse 48:

- "eternal stillness": literally, "silence that stretched for ages and then an age"

Verse 59:

- "swallowed": "devoured"

Verse 60:

- "cast aside": literally, "intentionally lose"

Verse 63:

- "abyss": "endless chasm"

29

Commentary & Analysis
Chapter 6

Chapter 6 contains what is probably the most heavily damaged portion of this entire scroll. There are several portions of this chapter that were slightly damaged and a couple of very large sections they were quite heavily damaged. One particular section even bears singe marks as if it had been slightly burned at some time in history, though I assure you, dear reader, that it was not damaged during the attack on our site in Romania. The damage is quite unfortunate because just as we saw in chapter 5, chapter 6 contains quite a unique tale as Simon finds himself within the Temple of the Lord. But that Temple of the Lord seems to be contained within Noah's Ark, a bit of fantastical imagery. That is truly unique because that piece of imagery has never been seen anywhere else in any portion of the world in any other text or scroll that has ever been found by anyone. This is further evidence of the truly historical nature and extreme importance of these documents that we unearthed.

The text begins with Simon following the Son of Man into the temple, and unfortunately there are several small portions of the scroll that have been destroyed in this section. Simon's consternation is clearly evident in the portions of text that we have, however. He is quite dismayed to be walking to the temple and seeing every animal from upon the entire face of the Earth contained within it, even those animals that were considered unclean. Although the unclean nature of the animals presented in this text is quite reminiscent of Peter's vision in the book of Acts when the sheet of animals is lowered before him, the imagery surrounding this Temple within the Ark that contains pairs of every animal on the Earth is quite extraordinary. Simon is clearly conveying through this revelation that everything that the Lord has created is worthy of being saved and is worthy of coming before God within the temple. That is a truly unique idea to be presented by anyone in the first century. Even going beyond what Peter was saying through his own revelation in the book of Acts, this imagery seems to open wide the freedom that those in Christ experience.

The Witness of the Lord shows up almost immediately in this chapter in verse 7 when he is already inside the Temple and watching the Son of Man and Simon approach. He bears witness to everything that happens within the temple, but as is shown at the end of the chapter, he himself is a false witness who changes the testimony that he is receiving.

As a hush falls throughout the temple, all of the animals pay attention to what the Lord is about to say, except for the raven. This is an interesting use of the raven in this revelation. It is of course a raven that Noah released from the ark that failed to bring back signs of land, but ravens are found throughout the Bible. Their imagery is not always consistent, however. In some cases the raven is considered a symbol of death; in other cases it is valued because it seems to have a premonition of death and be able to prey upon the weak and newly deceased. In other instances, however, especially in the book of 1 Kings, it is ravens that bring Elijah food to eat to keep him alive. The use of the raven in this revelation is much closer to the way in which it was used during Noah's time as one searching for death at the end of God's judgment.

In verse 17 the Son of Man opens the Law and the Prophets, which is usually considered to be the first several books of the Bible. The text from which the Lord reads, however, is almost nonexistence within the text of the Bible that we have today. Verse 18 talks about a message being sent against Jacob. Verse 19 talks about bricks falling down and being rebuilt with river stones. Verse 20 talks about ash trees being cut down and replaced by cedars. Verse 21 talks about someone going down to the king of Judah and proclaiming a prophetic message to the king. None of these instances and recitations from history are lumped together in quite this arrangement through any of the rest of the Bible. It is especially unfortunate that a large portion of text from this section of the chapter is missing. Perhaps if we had more of this recitation of this history we could better place what exactly it is that is being referenced by these snippets of time periods. Verse 36, however, begins a portion of scripture that we are quite familiar with, and that is the Sermon on the Mount. Specifically the Beatitudes as they are referenced in Matthew 5:3-10. This portion of the Beatitudes, however, that is recited by Simon differs in a couple significant ways from what is seen in the Book of Matthew. First, this recitation of the Beatitudes is far shorter than what we commonly know in the Book of Matthew. Second, there are some unique differences, especially in verses 37 and 39. In verse 37, Simon's text refers to those who are hungry or thirsty and the Lord giving them food and drink. That is specifically a physical need and a physical request that is granted. However in Matthew's Beatitudes the people are hungry, but they thirst for righteousness not for water. And in verse 39, those who are meek were given an inheritance in the kingdom of God. But in Mathew's version of the Beatitudes those who are meek are given inheritance of the kingdom on Earth. That may be nothing more than a slight difference in semantics, or it could be a completely different interpretation of doctrine and tradition.

Following this recitation of the scrolls, the raven returns with a freshly plucked olive leaf, and the implication is that the storm outside that was the Lord's judgment upon the Earth has subsided. Unfortunately we once again have a large section of text that is missing. Judging from the change in narrative, we can probably say that the Lord's Temple, which was also Noah's Ark, came to rest on a mountaintop and that the Witness of the Lord exited the Temple and Simon followed him. Beginning in verse 54, the Witness of the Lord is seen to be shaking out the words of the Lord from the Scrolls on which he had written them. However Simon comes upon them and finds that they have been corrupted. They are not a true representation of what he and the Witness of the Lord had seen within the Lord's Temple.

When Simon and the Witness of the Lord finally reach the base of the mountain they are greeted by the people from every tribe of Israel. What happens next is a clear reference to the children of Israel being fed manna in the desert. However when the Witness of the Lord shakes out the words of the Lord upon the ground, it makes the people sick. This reinforces the idea that the Witness is not a true witness to what he sees because the truth would not make those people sick. Interestingly, even though the people become sick from eating the words that are given to them by the Witness they go out and gather more of these words to eat them later. Though Simon tries to persuade them otherwise, they only laugh at him and keep the words for themselves.

△△△

Verse 9

- "defiling": existing in opposition to God

Verse 13:

- "a great stillness": literally "deep silence"

Verse 16:

- "the storm of the judgment of the Lord": alternatively "the storm of God's wrath"

Verse 17:

- "transformed": "made new"; the same word used to describe butterflies emerging

Verse 42:

- "covered by": alternatively, when used as an active verb, "blinded by"

Verse 54:

- "shook out": literally, "dropped from the folds and upon the road at his feet"

Verse 61:

- "craving": literally "salivating"

Verse 63:

- "retching": literally "dry heaving"

30

Commentary & Analysis
Chapter 7

Chapter 7 is interesting for two specific points. This chapter is one of the shorter ones throughout the entire revelation, and it also contains a very direct and simple message of transition from one portion of the Revelation to the next. After watching the Witness spread his corrupted version of the Lord's word upon the ground, Simon calls out to the Lord to stop this abomination. It is not the Lord who answers, however, but it is the First Man. Accompanying the First Man is the death and destruction of leprosy upon his body as well as the scouring winds that seem to be coming from the Lord himself. Those scouring winds remove all trace of the landscape and then reveal the Temple of the Lord. The temple itself, however, is also destroyed and scattered to the four corners of the world. We see the Temple's interior revealed to us all the way down to the Holy of Holies and the Ark of the Covenant. They are all blown away by the scouring wind of the Lord's blowing sand.

There is a message of cleansing throughout this chapter that is clearly shown by the Lord wiping away all traces of the landscape and of the Temple. It is very reminiscent of Noah's flood and the cleansing of the world of all the unrighteous. Interestingly, however, what is revealed by this cleansing is not a further righteousness of the Lord but the Witness himself standing at the center of that cleansing and continuing to spread his corrupted words. The Witness seems to be taking advantage of the Lord's sandstorm by tearing apart the corrupted words of the Scrolls that he had written and scattering them upon the winds, using the Lord's own cleansing wind to spread more corruption.

Upon watching the destruction of the Scrolls and the scattering of their words upon the wind, Simon tears at his clothes and cries out to the Lord to stop the blasphemy. It is not clear which blasphemy he is referring to, however, whether it is the blasphemy of the destruction of the Scrolls or the blasphemy of the corrupted words that had originally been written upon them. The resounding of the hundred trumpets brings a close to everything that has happened in this chapter, and it is a natural transition to the next chapter where Simon sees the world come back to life.

△△△

Verse 1:

- "fell to the ground": literally "prostrated myself upon the earth"

Verse 2:

- "wipe away": literally "obliterate"

Verse 5:

- "flies": literally "death insects," interpreted here as "flies"

Verse 7:

- "wooded desert": alternatively, "forested desert" or "lush desert"; the wording is vague and contradictory

Verse 9:

- "raging wind": alternatively, "wind of judgment"; the words can be interpreted as natural or supernatural, depending on the context

Verse 10:

- "for all eternity": literally, "until the end of days"; also in Verse 15

Verse 11:

- "dig up": literally "churn up"; the verb is an

odd choice because it is more commonly used in describing water than sand; the same verb is used in Verses 12, 13, and 14, which are rendered "dug up" and "blown away" respectively

Verse 21:

- "took no heed": literally, "was disturbed not by them"

31

Commentary & Analysis
Chapter 8

The narrative that is delivered in chapter 8 is one of great despair. It begins with Simon in complete darkness. He has torn his robes, called out to the Lord, heard the trumpet blasts, and been left by himself in that darkness. Interestingly, Simon is not a person who remains still for very long, and within moments he begins walking through the darkness until he sees a light upon the horizon. There is nothing in the text to indicate where the light came from, whether it's a natural light or something being supernaturally imposed upon the blind beggars that Simon comes upon. Each of those beggars, however, has received a portion of the Torah scroll that the Witness was scattering upon the wind, and he is copying it, likely to be further distributed around the world. This causes great distress for Simon who tries to stop them from their work, but to no avail.

When physically trying to stop them does not work, Simon begins preaching. His preaching, however, is interesting for the fact that this is nothing more than merely a recitation of the history of Israel. Again, this sermon seems to imply that Simon is speaking to a Jewish population, reminding them of where they have come from and the rich history that is behind them. Throughout his preaching, Simon goes back to the Exodus from Egypt, moves forward to the kingdom of David, on to the succession of Kings who were both followers of the Lord and rebels from the Lord, and finally to the birth of Jesus.

If the sermon is as much a recitation of the history of Israel and the Jewish population, then the reaction the blind beggars have to hearing Jesus's name is quite a pointed rebuke at the Jewish rejection of Jesus's death and resurrection. Simon seems to be pointedly saying that it was Jesus who brought death to the Jewish nation that rejected him. Interestingly, it is the appearance of the First

Man who then brings resurrection to the blind beggars representing the Jewish state. This is a clear analogy to Jesus being the first and the last, the Alpha and the Omega, the Adam and the Christ.

That interpretation would seem to be the most likely given the circumstances of the writing of this text, but there is a second interpretation. The blind beggars are doing nothing more than copying down the corrupted word that the Witness had torn and scattered upon the wind. To have the First Man resurrect those blind beggar and to then have them continue their copying of untruths is quite intriguing. This could perhaps mean that there is no stopping the corruption that Simon has seen of the Lord's word, which would seem to track with the overall negative portrayal that this particular Revelation leaves of and for the people who are receiving it. Alternatively this passage could mean that no matter what someone might do to stop the spread of the Gospel, whether it is the slaying of those who are spreading it or the corruption of the word itself, that spreading of the word of God will continue. That is a more optimistic interpretation of this passage that doesn't quite bear out with the tone of the rest of the Revelation, but it should still be considered. Or as a third alternative, because this chapter ends with Simon being taken up into Heaven, it could be that there is simply no stopping the corruption that is being done to the Lord's word and the only escape is to go directly to God.

It is also quite intriguing that the last several verses of this chapter have Simon trying to stop the First Man from bringing resurrection to the blind beggars who are corrupting the word of the Lord. Three times, Simon declares that the beggars are not copying the words of the Lord, and three times the First Man simply says that the words shall endure. Again this can be taken as either a positive or negative statement, but a negative interpretation is the more likely one considering the overall negative tone of Simon's entire Revelation. That would seem to imply that it is a bad thing that even though the beggars are being brought back to life through the First Man's resurrection attempts and prayer that they will simply continue to spread their misinformation.

△△△

Verse 1:

- "surrounded": literally "enveloped"

Verse 4:

- "an age": "yom": an unspecified period of time with a definite end

Verse 5:

- "light": "ohr," a physical light with a divine origination

Verse 6:

- "faded": literally "dim"

Verse 9:

- "quill": "kulmus"; most often a turkey feather or reed

Verse 11:

- "copying it": literally "acting as 'sofer'" (or scribe); the inclusion of the "acting as" verb in this sentence is pointed because a "sofer" is usually someone highly trained in transcribing the word of the Lord; these blind beggars, however, are merely "acting as" "sofers," not truly trained in the discipline

Verse 13:

- "stupor": literally "katanuxis" or "deep sleep"; again in verse 17

Verse 30:

- "chastened": literally "mustar" or "disciplined"

32

Commentary & Analysis
Chapter 9

This chapter marks a significant turning point in this revelation. This is, in fact, the final segment of the entire Revelation, and almost the entirety of the remaining chapters takes place within the throne room of God. This final segment of the revelation starts out as an uplifting entrance into the throne room of God and slowly degenerates over the next five chapters to show the desolation of the ends of times upon the Earth.

This chapter picks up with the Lord God Almighty placing Simon in the throne room of Heaven. While that would be unique enough in its own right, it is the way that the Lord God Almighty interacts with Simon in the throne room that makes it such an incredible experience. That includes the language that Simon is using to refer to God in this segment of the revelation. It is with chapter 9 that Simon begins referring to God with the phrase the Lord God Almighty. That phrase can be translated many different ways but it basically means the One, the Creator, the Beginning and the End, and the single most powerful being in all of the world. All of those interpretations of this one Hebrew word would be correct, and that is why I have chosen to render it as the Lord God Almighty. It distinctly refers to someone far greater than anyone who has been shown in this Revelation up to this point, and that can only be God Himself.

As incredible as that usage of the phrase Lord God Almighty might be, it is also unique because Simon is not using the typical Hebrew name of God as "Yahweh" (specifically, "YHWH"). That marks a distinct turning point during the first century as people begin referring to God as an omniscient being instead of as the name of God, Yahweh. The significance of this find within this Revelation cannot be overstated because this lends credence to theories about when that change in language for followers of the Way really began to take place. Now we know because of this Revelation that the change in language began happening soon after the destruction of the temple in Jerusalem, sometime after 70 CE.

Simon begins his time in the Throne Room of Heaven by bowing his head and not looking upon the Lord. While that is typical of anyone entering into the temple or coming close to the presence of God, what is so unique is God lifting Simon's head so that he might actually see God walking through. This image is once again quite reminiscent of an Old Testament story when God passed before Elijah as Elijah was hiding in the crook of the rock. What is so uniquely different about this instance however is that Simon does not need to hide himself from the Lord as Elijah did but is allowed to see God walking through the throne room and sitting upon the throne and before the banquet table.

That banquet table itself is also quite unique to any other imagery that might be found within the Bible and among other texts that have been uncovered in the last 2,000 years. Though we have in the gospels the stories of Jesus referring to the "banquet table" that the Lord was setting for his followers in Heaven, this is the first place in all of recorded Biblical literature where that banquet table is actually seen. The banquet table itself is actually quite unique as it affords God and the creatures who reside with him in the Throne Room a window upon the world for them to view the comings and goings of people. We see God and the creatures in the Heavenly throne room and Simon all watching people live their lives, and we see that everything that is revealed of the earth is being reviewed by everyone who stands with God. The theological implications of this within the Revelation are staggering. Are we meant to interpret from this passage that anyone who resides with God in Heaven is privy to details like this upon the Earth? Or are we meant to interpret this as revealing something of Simon's unique nature in this Revelation that God is sharing this particularly with him and that no one else in Heaven would ever get to experience something like this? These are theological questions probably best reserved for later discussions.

Almost immediately upon beginning to view the comings and goings of people upon the Earth, we see the entrance of a shadow upon the land,

and that shadow is soon revealed to be the Witness who has been corrupting the word of the Lord throughout this entire journey in the Revelation. Harkening back to the story of the Garden of Eden from this Revelation, as the Witness moves across the land people's hearts become heavy, and they realize that something is missing within their lives. Interestingly, that emptiness affects all of the first-born children of both Jews and gentiles who begin living out their lives as empty shells upon the Earth. Though this is clearly supposed to harken back to the story of the Angel of Death in the Exodus, it is puzzling in this instance that that emptiness would be reaching everyone, whether they follow the Lord or not.

The burden that is weighing down the people upon the Earth is soon shifted, however, as the First Man begins his journey upon the Earth as a welcoming creature attempting to invite people back to God. Some people do that, but very few of them. Those who actually do approach the First Man are quickly rewarded, and the chapter ends, in a bit of wording paralleling the opening chapters of this Revelation, on an uplifting note as Simon declares that everything the First Man was doing was good.

∆∆∆

Verse 1:

- "Seat of honor": "King's throne" or "judgment throne" or "judgment seat"

Verse 3:

- "lifted my face high": Literally "uplifted me"

Verse 4:

- "to witness": "to observe"

Verse 5:

- "bowed": "prostrated" themselves

Verse 6:

- "did not allow it": Literally "refused it from," but that translation seemed to go against the image of a loving God, so I did not use it

Verse 8:

- "breathed upon": Literally "breathed the spirit into"

Verse 11:

- "shadow": Literally "perfect darkness," but rendered here as "shadow" to remain consistent with the following verses that are the correct word for "shadow"

Verse 16:

- "the people": Literally "the chosen"

Verse 20:

- "Then": "After a time"

Verse 22:

- "Stepped away": Literally "side-stepped"

Verse 23:

- "Burned": "ached"

Verse 24:

- "Lit again": "rekindled"

33

Commentary & Analysis
Chapter 10

Unfortunately this chapter, like so many before it, has been damaged by the seeds of time. The only positive thing we can say about the damage to this section of the Revelation is that each individually damaged piece is minor compared to some of the extensive damage that has come before. At most, we are probably only missing a handful of verses between all of the smaller parts that have been damaged throughout this chapter. As always, those have been marked accordingly.

Though the previous chapter ended on such an uplifting note, that changes almost immediately as chapter 10 begins. Those souls that were reborn for the Lord are set upon by the evil one and his minions. In this case it is an infestation of fleas upon the world. Again this harkens back to the Exodus and the curses that were called upon pharaoh and his people. However though we are missing a small portion of text between verses 5 and 7, it can be easily understood that it is the First Man who is standing and holding back the tide of the fleas upon the world. As he speaks the word of the Lord into the oncoming onslaught of the curse, they are held back until finally one of the hosts of Heaven declares that it has begun. It is at that point that the infestation is released upon the world.

Just as with the Exodus story, this curse afflicts everyone and everything upon the world. There is no place that the fleas do not seem to be able to go. However unlike the purpose of the curse upon Pharaoh's people, the purpose of the curse of these fleas seems to be that people's hearts have become hard to the Lord. There is an interesting theological implication by that curse turning people further from God. Was that the original intention? If so it begs the question as to what God really intended as the conclusion of this curse. As before with such theologically weighted implications it is probably best to leave that discussion for another time.

It is the First Man once again who is standing in the time of darkness. As shown by verse 23, the First Man continues to speak the word of the Lord into this curse. The result however is that the people cast aside the Law and the Prophets, and they stop their prayers to God. Instead of turning back to God, they turn their backs on Him and pursue the unrighteous. No matter what the people do, however, that does not change what the First Man's purpose is upon the world. He stands alone proclaiming the word of God, and it is his prayer that moves the Lord to action. With a mighty clap of thunder, the Lord ceases the curse upon the Earth, and all of the fleas fall dead. The chapter ends on a positive note that all was good. Unfortunately the conclusion of this chapter stands in stark contrast to the conclusion of chapter 11.

∆∆∆

Verse 1:

- "Shining beacon": similar to the word for "lighthouse," but meant to imply a light

source in the desert; rendered here as "shining beacon"

Verse 3:

- "The new age": Literally "the second age"

Verse 13:

- "Hearts grew hard": Literally "turned away"

Verse 16:

- "The very seas": Literally "the five seas," but
  as there are not only five seas, rendered here
  as "the very seas" to avoid confusion

Verse 29:

- "Lusts": Literally "debauchery"

34

Commentary & Analysis
Chapter 11

As chapter 10 is covering a physical curse upon the people, so chapter 11 seems to turn to a spiritual curse upon those who reject the Lord. This chapter begins with a pause in the action. The world is still for several ages, but even in this stillness the First Man is not content to do nothing. He weeps upon the ground, and it is the Witness that grows up from his tears. This is a unique Witness, however, compared to the Witness that we have seen through most of this Revelation. This Witness does not at first seem to be corrupting the word of the Lord but seems instead to be spreading His truthful word upon the Earth. Even Simon seems to find this uplifting as his heart leaps for joy to hear the testimony of the Witness.

That joy, however, is quickly subdued as Simon turns to the Lord and sees that the Lord is weeping. That weeping is unique throughout this chapter because it is probably the greatest show of tears and agony that the Lord expresses anywhere in scripture for He is crying throughout the rest of this chapter for what He is seeing transpire upon the Earth.

The Witness goes out into the world preaching about the Lord's return and bringing together a flock of followers around him who are equally excited for the Lord's return. As the chapter continues, these people turn their faces to the heavens and await the Lord's return, which does not happen. Even with the Witness shouting to the heavens, "Behold the Lord," it does not happen. As with much of scripture we find the repetition of the holy number 3 as the witness proclaims three times that the people should behold the Lord coming down from the heavens. Finally, upon that last time of not seeing the Lord's return, the people turn as one away from the Lord, and this is their final rejection of God as expressed in this Revelation. It is also the greatest show of sorrow that the Lord offers in this Revelation, or in any Biblical text. He is truly weeping for the lost upon the world.

The chapter concludes as a mirror image of chapter 10, this time with the Lord weeping and His tears flowing upon the Earth and Simon's declaration that it was not good.

△△△

Verse 2:

- "At the center of the Earth": Literally "core of the Earth"

Verse 6:

- "fell upon": "wetted"

Verse 7:

- "Shadow": "pitch darkness," as in Chapter 9; rendered here as "shadow" to maintain consistency with the overall narrative of this chapter

Verse 9:

- "Whispered": More broadly interpreted as "spoke delicately and deliberately"; also in verses 10, 11, and 12.

Verse 13:

- "Wind": "spirit"

Verse 19:

- "Sky" and "skies": Literally "heavens"

Verse 20:

- "Darkness": "shadow"

Verse 21:

- "He would not hear them": alternatively translated "He refused to hear them," but rendered here as "would not here them" to maintain consistency of interpretation regarding God's known character.

Verse 29:

- "Did not come": alternatively translated "could not come"; also in verses 31 and 34.

35

Commentary & Analysis
Chapter 12

Chapter 12 is a relatively short chapter, and the story it tells is a relatively direct story. In fewer than two dozen sentences Simon tells how the people of the world turn their backs upon God and become soulless, hollow shells. The chapter begins with life continuing on as if the Lord had never been. People are going about their daily lives, but they are slowly losing their souls and losing their very essences because they have lost the Lord. This becomes manifest finally in the blood dripping from their eyes as they go about their daily tasks, but none of them seem to realize it.

The scene in heaven is equally heart-wrenching as the Lord spreads His arms above the table and beckons the people to return to Him. They do not, and what follows is probably the second shortest verse in all of scripture when Simon writes those three words: "The Lord wept." The scene continues with a graphic account of the peoples of the world turning upon the First Man, trampling him, cutting up his body, and sending the pieces to the 12 tribes of Israel. This is meant as a not-so-subtle reference to Judges 19 when a Levite cut up into 12 pieces the body of his dead concubine and sent the pieces throughout Israel.

As this chapter concludes, the Lord turns his back upon the people and Simon declares that it is not good.

∆∆∆

Verse 1:

- "Turned their hearts": alternatively, "sought"

Verse 2:

- "Corruption": alternatively, "deception"

Verse 9:

- "Beckoned": alternatively translated "ordered," but rendered here as the less common "beckoned." Also in verse 10.

Verse 10:

- "Was calling them": Literally "directed them"

Verse 18:

- "Turned His back upon": also "rejected," but the root denotes a physical action, so here rendered as "turned His back"

36

─────

Commentary & Analysis
Chapter 13

This is the final chapter of this revelation of Simon, and the dramatic differences could not be more pronounced between this and the Revelation of John that we currently have in the Christian New Testament than what is revealed by this final chapter. So unlike John's revelation is this revelation of Simon, and so starkly shown, as this chapter ends on one of the most despairing notes. This chapter shows God abandoning the Earth, leaving his Temple, and the Heavenly creatures turning away from all of creation. We see Simon left to himself for what he describes as an eternity, and the entire Revelation ends on this note of despair.

As the chapter begins, all of Heaven is in silence, and the Lord leaves His throne room. Interestingly, it is His shadow cast upon the Earth that actually brings death to His creation. It is from that death that the people of the world try to bring themselves back to life. In a scene reminiscent of "Brave New World," the people of the Earth take the remnants of their life without the Lord and turn that around to say that what is bad is actually good, that what is death is actually life. Though it seems to be a valiant effort, Simon's Revelation makes clear that the people are left with no spiritual life. They are left with no God to worship. And that lack of spiritual renewal is what leads them to depart off the edge of the Lord's table.

After spending an eternity alone in the Lord's Temple, Simon awakens to find himself returned to the Tabernacle in the desert. The angels have dispersed, and the four doors are wide open to the world outside. Simon knows what he must do with this Revelation, that he must take it to all the peoples of the world. His fear at the Revelation's conclusion is palpable as the final verse of the entire book is a warning that what has been revealed must never come to pass. And so ends the Revelation of Simon, the son of Cuphythis.

ΔΔΔ

Verse 2:

- "Darkness": Alternatively, "hole" or "emptiness"

Verse 4:

- "Did not live": Literally "left without a soul"; also in verses 5, 6, and 7

Verse 7:

- "Walked upon": Alternatively, "danced upon," but the context implies sorrow, not joy

Verse 10:

- "Cast aside": Literally, "abandoned"

- "Word": Literally "truth," but translated here as "word" to remain in context with the nearby verses

Verse18:

- "Empty": The word actually has two inter-pretations, one implying "silently empty" and the other implying "empty because of abandonment"; rendered here as simply "empty" to avoid any confusion

Verse 19:

- "Silence": Literally, "stillness"

37

Commentary & Analysis
Epilogue

This revelation is an absolutely stunning find. It provides a deeper window into the early Christians' lives and how they perceived the world. So much of what we know of later 1st-century Christian lives has unfortunately been lost to history. We have been able to piece together through conjecture and through the scant writings that we have and what we know from Roman, Greek, and Jewish sources unrelated to Christianity only the bare bones of how life was perceived at that time.

This Revelation is also so dramatically different from the one Revelation of John that still survives to this day. By comparing the two as nearly contemporary with each other we are getting a fuller view of the early Christians' perceptions on one of the most dramatic incidents in history, the destruction of the Jewish temple. Whereas the Revelation of John moves forward from that point and shows us God's redemption of all people on Earth, this Revelation of Simon provides a stark contrast, showing us God turning His back upon all people. I imagine we will be examining these texts side by side for many decades to come so that we can better understand and interpret the major theological implications of what these two men were saying to their contemporaries, as well as what they are saying to us today.

As I explained in my introduction, this Revelation of Simon is only one text among the dozens that I was able to smuggle out with me. I have maintained the integrity of these ancient scrolls as best I can without the support of my colleagues and while fearing for my life. I am using my time in the late hours of the night to painstakingly translate these texts as quickly as I can, but it is slow going. Though my knowledge of ancient languages is extensive, I must admit that I still find this as difficult as I find it exhilarating. Unfortunately, for my own safety I must continue to be on the move, and that means I am unable to devote all of my time and energy to this project as I would wish. I still do not understand why any group of people from anywhere in the world would not want this treasure trove of knowledge from the 1st century to be shared with everyone on Earth. This Revelation of Simon's has inspired and renewed my own faith in God. I can only imagine what it is doing for your faith, dear reader.

Please be patient with me as I work forward in my translations of these documents. I plan to move to another part of this beautiful country, and I do not know how quickly I can return to the work that has become the overriding passion of my life, the translation of and commentaries upon these texts. I trust the blessings of the Lord will fall upon you as they have fallen upon me. Until we meet again, God be with you.

H. Dean Fisher
*Photo by: John Kilker at
JohnJKilker.com*

H. Dean Fisher is author of the fantastic, the scientifically fictional, and the macabre. His fiction and photography has won awards at various conferences and competitions throughout the United States. He currently teaches in a mass communication department at a Christian university in Pennsylvania. His research interests include gender representation in videogame journalism; credibility in public relations and broadcasting; and mythological portrayals in media.

Books by H. Dean Fisher:

The Tales of Zhava series (young adult fantasy):

"The Initiate: Book 1"
"The Novice: Book 2"

"Bes" (children's chapter book, Fall 2022)

"The Jungle God" (science fiction)

"Medusa: Dawn of a Goddess" (mythological/urban fantasy, Spring 2022)

Website: www.hdeanfisher.com - sign up for the monthly newsletter
Facebook: www.facebook.com/SeventhBattlePublishing
Twitter: @HDeanFisher1
Instagram: HDeanFisher

www.ingramcontent.com/pod-product-compliance
Lightning Source LLC
Chambersburg PA
CBHW031009190726
48286CB00003BA/761